Cul de sac
MOON

Kimberley Clarke

ISBN 09-86500100

ISBN-13 978-0-9865001-0-7

PUBLISHER'S NOTE

This is a work of fiction. Names, characters, places and incidents either are the product of the author's overactive imagination or are used fictitiously, and any resemblance to actual persons, living or dead, events, or locales is entirely coincidental and all in your head.

Library and Archives Canada Cataloguing in Publication

Clarke, Kimberley

Cul De Sac Moon / Kimberley Clarke
I. Title

 Pink Wig Publishing

West Vancouver, British Columbia
V7S 3E5

For Donald, Maddison, Kelsey and Jet,
my only reasons.

Acknowledgements

Giant thank-yous and hugs go out to:

Karen Aitken and Ken Elphick (for their ready smiles and editing eyes)

Andree D'Andrea   (for being counsellor extraordinaire and keeping Addie honest and real)

Jan Hyslop (for being my friend for fifty years and having especially nimble fingers and mad computer skills)

Johnny Fly (former student and graphic visionary who pulled the cover right out of my brain and onto the page).

Cul de sac
MOON

1

"Whoa Addie! Get a load of what is going on in your driveway! Whose car is that and what exactly is your mother doing?" exclaims Sigge my shiny new best friend.

"Ohmigawd," I manage to choke out. "I have absolutely no idea Sig. It looks like this could be a wild and manic kind of day. Ooohboy. Sig, uh... sheesh! Do you think you could come over later maybe, like once I get to the bottom of this?"

I really don't like surprises. Someone always ends up crying and locked in the bathroom. They do at my house anyway. Most people like surprises and they wish for them, but not me. I am way too suspicious and nervous. So when I lay my eyes on the strange car in the driveway my teeth clench, my stomach drops and takes my breath with it.

A Pontiac Firebird looms in our driveway, a seemingly foreign luxury yacht to my eyes. Sleek shiny blue lines and blood red vinyl interior. We must have company. We never have anything new at our house.

I have to get rid of Sigge. It is still a little too early in our friendship for her to witness this weird action.

"I'll call you when things settle, okay Sig?" I say. *Oh man. This is so awkward.*

"Sure Addie. No problemo! I have to practice the piano anyway. Ciao for now!" Sigge chirps and smiles, but I think I see her wince as she says goodbye.

Sigge is very cool. I don't have to say much and she takes the hint. Like right now when the ancient weird ones are doing this photo shoot with the Polaroid camera my Dad bought new in the seventies, she toddles off as if they are the most normal parents in the world. And that is just one of the things that I like about her. Another thing is that I could tell her anything and she wouldn't even flinch. Like I could say that I wish I was the reason a song was written, a real song not a kazoo instrumental, and that I am really quite sentimental and unicorn rainbow mushy on the inside but it's way easier to be scratchy and irritable on the outside. Fewer questions to answer, fewer lies to tell. I could say that I talk to the moon and hope it can hear me and my wishes and Sigge would understand all of this because she is an amazing artist and she is just that way, you know, accepting. She is a nice change from my old best friend, Lindsay, but I will get to THAT later. Right now I need to figure out how to not get involved with this wacky nonsense that the parents have dreamed up and how to create a logical explanation for their bizarre behaviour. Rationalizing their nonsense is becoming a nightmare.

My mother is stretched out on the roof of the car as if she is a panther or something. She is pouting and purring at my dad and the camera.

"Addie, my beautiful little ginger kitty. Come up here and join me. Daddy can take a picture of both of us, together on the roof of the car. It'll be cute. It will be something I can show to my grandkids one day. Right Sweetie?" She says as she winks at my dad.

I can tell mom is a little "altered". She is way too happy.

"And don't forget, Dee, that you can say to those grand kiddies, 'See if you can guess which of these twin beauties is your grandmother. Come on Addie, upsie, daisy'."

My dad winks at my mom and I am so grossed out. He still thinks she is pretty cute after all this time and all and that's cool, so I guess I am pretty lucky that way but I don't know. You'd think he would smarten up and notice that she's always a little tipsy and cranky and weird, and like maybe do something about it, but hey. What do I know? Like how do you tell your dad to maybe notice that his wife, my mother is an off the rails dope fiend and alcoholic? Where is a parent manual when you need one?

"Yoo-hoo Addie. Space girl! I'll help you up. Give me your hand. Step on the window edge and I'll yank." Mom says this as if it is the most normal thing in the world. Of course I will climb up on the roof of a brand new to us car and have a picture taken with my mother all decked out in some wild orange and blue polka-dotted Capri-pant creation from 1975. Why does she save this stuff? She's all smiley and surrounded by a cloud of her nasty drugstore perfume, Taboo, that she saves for special occasions. It just smells like big, big, trouble to me.

"Just a second, would ya," I snarl as I pull my hand away. "Whose car is this? Aren't they going to be a little

5

pissed to find our lousy footprints all over their minty paint job?" I say to my father as he puffs himself up to almost double his normal ego size.

"No Miss Adelaide they won't. I am the proud new owner of this grand specimen of vehicular transportation. Your Uncle Harold was able to wrangle a deal on two of these awesome beasts so I stepped up to the plate and said yesseroonie to a new car. So what do you think? Pretty nice, huh?"

"But Dad, you don't even drive! What's the point?"

Uncle Harold. It figures. My Uncle Harold is not my real uncle. I am just supposed to call him that. He's my dad's best friend. Uncle Harold was married to Auntie Mame. She wasn't my aunt really either. Harold is my father's idol. He has disposable income because they don't have kids. Harold is loaded, with money and alcohol. I always thought it was weird that Auntie Mame's name was Mame. She was really badly burned and scarred in a fire when she was a kid. People's names sometimes slay me. I think names have vibrations and make you into whatever they say you are. So "Mame" and my mom used to talk a lot about the baby that Mame lost. It would have had the same birthday as me they said. They never said the word pregnant in front of me. I thought that was weird even when I was little. They always said "p-g". It took me a while

6

to realize they weren't saying pig. I could never figure out how pigs played a role in her losing a baby, except that maybe Harold and Mame lived on a farm or that Mame was allergic to pork.

Mame kept a trunk filled with hand-knitted baby clothes and when she had drunk just enough gin she would weep and drag me into some locked dark room to look at all these sad pink and yellow baby clothes. All I could think of at the time was that this was a serious waste of good doll clothes being kept in an old smelly cedar trunk. Empathy is not a word in my vocabulary. Sympathy either. Mame died from complications from alcoholism. Starvation I think. It is so tragic because she and Harold ordered Chinese in all of the time and just let it sit on the counter in their kitchen without touching it. Such a gigantic waste. They should have called me. I love Chinese food. Mame could have had decent meals all of the time if she had just walked into her kitchen. Now Uncle Harold and his girlfriends come around on Sundays and pretend to eat dinner with us. They push roast beef around on their plates and wash what little manages to find their mouths down with the scotch that my father inelegantly pours for them. You'd think my mom would learn. You 'd think my dad would care. You think they would notice the foreshadowing.

7

"Addie. ADDIE! Where did you go? Are you astral projecting again dear? Did you hear that one Dee? Astral projecting. Gawd. I kill myself…. Addie? Hop on yer pop onto the top! Did you get my Dr. Seuss reference there Addie? I'm just killin' today girls. Up, up dear! Your mother is waiting." Dad says this as he aims the camera at my mother's cleavage.

"You know Dad, I think I'd like to go and change and put my backpack in my room. You know, basic after school stuff? You and mom go ahead and amuse yourselves. Point and shoot, Dad. Just point and shoot."

"There is absolutely no need to make fun of this camera Addie. It takes THE best pictures. Always has. Just you wait and see." Dad points and pretends to shoot the thing at me. My nose wrinkles in response.

"Hurry Cliff, my cheeks are getting sore from all of this smiling. If Addie wants to be an old stick in the muck then that's her business. Come on Cliffie, I'm waiting." Mom licks her orange sticky gloss lips, and then bares her teeth.

I guess this is her version of a smile.

As I shuffle my way to our back door, I notice a few of the neighbours on our cul-de-sac looking out of their kitchen windows at the Former Old Top Model moment taking place in our driveway. I know they are shaking their heads. It's not the first time we Sinclairs have supplied the neighbourhood with second class entertainment and I am sure it won't be the last.

2

The house is quiet now with mom and dad both out on the driveway drooling on the car. I like it this way. Just the hum of the furnace fan, the rhythmic drip of water in the kitchen sink as background music, and me. Peace and white-noise quiet.

I grab an orange pop out of the fridge and head for my room. My bedroom is my refuge these days. It smells like me, it feels like me, it performs magic for me. In my room the moon is always full and glacial blue. It hangs in my window and waits for all my wishes and dreams. It winks when I tell it secrets or sing it songs with moon in the lyrics. It is my own private star. I drape myself across my bed sideways and hang my head upside down and I gaze at the Sea of Tranquility and wish for some. The blood rushes to my head and my ears throb

10

like bongos. I also wish that I would get the part of ethereal Lucy in our school's drama production of Dracula and that my dad would stop wearing chocolate brown velour jump-suits. I wish for stuff all of the time. I don't get everything that I wish for though, just what I truly need it seems.

I wish my mom would get a grip on her party-girl behaviour. A big grip. A major grip. A total handle. I wish. So, so what if it's not really the moon. So what if it is only the street lamp in the lane behind our house. It's always there, it's always bright and full and it always listens patiently to no matter what I tell it. It never leaves the room in the middle of my sentences to have a little lie down.

The new-to-us car thing is confusing. We rarely have new stuff in this family. Not that we don't need any. Or that we can't afford it, it's just that my parents seem to have chosen an era and have frozen us all into it.

I think they chose 1972. According to this month's issue of Stylemag we are completely in style again, forty odd years later. We may be in style but our stuff is really old. Which brings me back to the car. Not only am I confused, but I am a little nervous because it must mean something. I sit up and let the blood run back into the rest of my body. I take a big gulp of my soda and look at the clock.

11

Sigge's piano practice must be over by now, it's 4:30. I've got to call her but I am still a little dizzy. Equilibrium is so elusive.

I have to tell you, Sigge is a very enthusiastic person. Everything is exciting and interesting to her. She bubbles and giggles and appreciates and boy can she ever be annoying. She drives me a little goofy sometimes but we get along. She kinda adopted me at the beginning of September this year. It took me a while to adjust to her zestiness but it is kind of infectious. She is also an amazing artist. Her mom is an architect and her dad is a social worker. He makes "kitchen art" as a hobby. Coffee mugs and sugar bowls, that kind of thing. She has a brother too. Bernerd. I have no idea if he makes art as well but I do know he is in drama at our school. He's older and has a reputation of being a total "Ber-nerd." I have only met him a couple of times and ooh boy yeah, so far his rep is not far from wrong. He wears a cape, he drives a black and chrome Italian scooter and has a crazy set of grey laser eyes that look right through you. He seems like the kind of guy who'd try to buy X-ray glasses from the back of antique comic books. A total geek-o-rama.

Before I pick up my phone to call Sigge it rings.

"Hello?" I say knowing full well it's Sigge and her enthusiasm calling.

"Okay Addie. What's the deal? What have you learned? When, where, why the new wheels?" ran-on Sig. "Don't disappoint me with a lame I haven't got a clue answer. I have been playing Sonatina in C for the last forty-five minutes and playing is a very loose term for what I was doing to that poor piece of music because I was so preoccupied with the idea of an almost new car and that you are on the verge of driver-dom and everything. The music was glad that I stopped butchering it I am sure. Soooooooooo? Quest-que C'est?"

"Like do you ever breathe when you talk Sig?" I say and take a really big breath of my own, for good measure. "It seems, my friend, that the giant sparkly blue car really does belong to the Sinclair clan. I am not completely clear on why exactly, but I'm sure I'll find out later from the latter day aging Twiggy and her crushed velvet not-so-boy-toy."

"Oh come on Addie. Forget them. You must be a kind of excited. A new car. An almost driver's license. A perfect date-magnet combo. Tell me you haven't been sitting in the driver's seat yet. I'll be really choked if you have actually sat in the car without me. I am going to be the absolutely most excellent passenger you have ever seen. Don't you see Addie? You've got to admit that that car is completely drive-in amazing, well if there were any drive-ins anymore. Just think how good you will look behind the wheel of that baby. Just think how cool I will look as your ever-faithful sidekick passenger. Sixteen is only a month away Miss. You could be driving that puppy before we know it!"

"Oh, um, Sig," I try to edge into the conversation that Sigge is having with herself.

"Oh Addie, I can see it all now. We'll cruise to Junior's Burger Barn and stink up the ruby red interior with fried onions. It'll be so great. I can hardly, I mean, I guess YOU can hardly wait to get your license now, right?" Sigge slid to a close.

"Good grief, Sig. I just saw the darn thing. Your creative visualization classes have really paid off haven't they?" I sneer.

"There is no need for your cynicism Addie. Visualizing works. Maybe you should try it sometime. You'll see just how effective it can be." Sigge says somewhat breathlessly.

I don't think this is the exact time to tell her about the full moon in my room, so I just let her go on.

"Addie this is so exciting. Ohmigaawd. You. You are on the verge of true driver hood. I can't wait to get in the front seat of that blue beauty. I'm coming over right after dinner. I'll bring my ipod. We'll sit in the car, listen to tunes, and pretend we are on a road trip, okay?"

See, Sigge is cute and enthusiastic and annoying. It's too bad Sigge's sixteenth birthday isn't before mine, then she could drive and I could be the perfect passenger because I come from a long line of passengers. My dad still doesn't have his license and I am not completely sure that I am ready for the open road just yet. But thinking about it opens up some new and potentially interesting possibilities for "visualization."

"Sure Sigge, whatever. See you after dinner."

Quietly, so that I can have the element of surprise on my side, I slither into the kitchen on my tube-socked feet. I am almost alone and it's still quiet. Mom and Dad must have come in while I was talking to Sigge. I can see into the living room from here and there is my dad in all his shiny glory reclining on his purple Zeeboy chair. He looks relaxed and very pleased with himself. In one hand he has a beer, and the other is clutching what look like a grey rubber stress ball. I love sneaking up on my dad. Especially when he is looking so satisfied. It doesn't seem fair that he can find a Zen moment and I can't. So, in my loudest stage projection voice, utilizing of course, my diaphragm, I bellow,

"Hey Dad, what's the deal with the new blue-wheeled sparkle unit and the splurge on film? Someone die and leave you a bundle of cash or something?"

I take great pleasure in his startle response.

"Adelaide Blanche! Just who do you think you are talking to? One of your spaced-out boy-crazed fiends? I'll have you know your mother and I bought the Pontiac so that she would have something nice to drive me around in. And second of all you are looking at the newest member of the Grimson's Men's Clothes Buying Team. I've got to look snappy inside and out of the store. Which reminds me. Here is a couple of bucks. Go and spruce yourself up with a little colour like you used to dress would you please? You look a little like a grieving widow these days. Your hamster die or something? Gawd I kill myself. Anyway, when you go to the mall don't forget to shop at Grimson's."

Dad sounds like he is going to break into an advertising jingle. What I thought was a stress ball turns out to be a soggy wad of money. He's been clutching it all afternoon. He peels off a bunch of limps bills from his fist with a smile so big that it drips off his face. I reach out, take the money, and cram it into my jeans pocket in one very smooth move.

"What no thank-you? Come here and crush me to your puny chest." He leans towards me arms outstretched.

"Daaad. Don't be so disgusting. I won't allow myself to be anointed with Brut. But yeah, here, I will definitely blow you a kiss. Thanks for the money and congrats on the job." I pull myself away.

"Thanks Missy. It's not Brut, by the way. It's called Indulge. The girls in the shoe department can't get enough of my heady scent. This stuff is as amazing as the ads say it is." and he winks.

Eeuuww. Nobody else's father talks to them this way. He is so creepy.

"Ohmigawd. You are so weird," I mumble and leave as quickly as I can for the sanctuary of my room. Conversation with Sigge is an immediate must. It will cleanse my brain. But first things first. Exactly how much moola did Dad give me?

I pull my sodden good fortune out of my pocket. This is crazy. I have never seen this much cash in my house before let alone in my own hands. I check the calendar to see if there is an actual full moon. Nope. I attribute his good mood and generosity to beer and ego.

18

I pick up the receiver of my phone and dial Sigg's number. We still have rotary dials at our house because touchtone and cell phones are viewed with suspicion. It has something to do with my mother's fear of lightning and simultaneously combusting during thunderstorms. Go figure. I am surprised to be as normal as I am.

The phone rings at Sigge's house seven times before someone picks up.

"Make this worth my while!" Bernerd growls into the phone. He's using the radio catch phrase that's supposed to win $100,000 if he's lucky and they call his number.

"You are such a geek. I can't believe that you think they'll call you. Is Sigge home?" I say.

"You know she is. She doesn't do or go anywhere without your approval your effin' highness." he snarls.

"Ya know Bernerd, I am impressed that you recognize greatness. Get your sister." I snap.

"Your wish is my ass, BL--ANCHE. Sigge! Queen BL-- ANCHE is on the phone." Bernerd hollers into the receiver.

He must know how much I hate that. Can you believe anyone is named Blanche in the twenty-first century? Geez.

"My namm--eee, comment savviiieee? Whazzup?" breathes Sigge into the receiver.

"We have won a trip to the mall. Giant weird one gave me, I repeat, gave me 200 bucks to buy a bunch of new and un-black clothes. Almost cool, huh?" I can hear a distinct pause on the other end of the line. It is almost as if Sig is thinking or something.

"He must be, uh, well, you know? He doesn't usually give you guys, oh never mind. Awesome. When do we leave? I have got to have a shower. Thursday night at Parkland Mall, Yeehaw. What are you going to get Addie? I'll be over in twenty. Is your mom going to drive us in the new car?" Sigge says with enthusiasm that refuses to die.

"I'll tell her that she has to. What else does she have to do except read her '5000 Ways to Cook with Liqueurs' recipe pamphlet?" I explain.

"I'll be over as soon as I am perfecto, Addie. Hang-up on three....One..."

Sigge always does this. She reminds me of when I was a little kid and how every minute and every second was spontaneous and fun. Not creepy and weird , like now.

"Three." we say and place our respective receivers into their cradles.

4

"Ohmigawd Mrs. Sinclair. Riding in this car is awesome. I feel like royalty being chauffeured to the mall like this. Thanks so much for the ride. I mean it. This sure beats taking the bus." bubbles Sigge.

"I know what you are saying Signe. This car does make you feel like a queen. That's exactly how Mr. Sinclair will feel every morning!" Sigge giggles like crazy at my mom's inadvertent joke.

"Sigge, you can stop sucking up to my mom. We're halfway to the mall. It's not as if she's going to dump us if we're not polite. Enough already."

"Adelaide Blanche, would it kill you to keep a little of your cynicism to yourself? Just because a person appreciates all the things that are done for them is no reason for you to ridicule and belittle them. I happen to agree with Sigge. This car does have a nice ride and feel to it. If I didn't have to keep my hands on the steering wheel I would be waving like the Queen of England too," my mom defends Sigge.

"You are wearing the right hat for it. Where did you unearth that creation?" I mutter. "Where does one find a white pleather Beatle cap these days?"

I am amazed that mom and Sigge can talk about nothing like this. It is as if they are having fun or something. I just can't seem to relax and enjoy their silliness. It just doesn't feel natural.

"Addie! Can you believe that we are here already? Thanks Mrs. Sinclair." Sigge saves my mom from yet another Addie harangue. "Where do you want us to meet you and at what time? I'll make sure we're not late. C'mon Addie let's go. Toodles, Mrs. S." Sigge grabs my arm and pulls us both out of the car and whips the door shut. My mom mouths "nine - thirty, right here" and pulls away.

After my mom slithers back into traffic I figure it's time to light into old friendly-puss Sigge.

23

"Could you have been any MORE annoying, Sig? Geez, it is not as if you were riding in a flippin' Mercedes. That would be something to gush about!" I hiss.

"Enough about me Addie. Let us concentrate on you and your money that is burning a hole in my pocket. Let's go shop-shop-shopping!"

I wonder if Sigge has a clue how cranky this day is making me?

****

In the middle of Parkland Mall is a very cool fountain. There is a little bridge over it and benches all around it. There are lots of tropical plants and flowers, birds of paradise and hibiscus in particular, and it's where everyone sits to meet friends, sip a latte or just hang out. Sig and I head for the fountain to plan our mall attack. Everyone from our school goes there to find out who is happening. Sig and I are about to sit when from across the bridge we hear,

"Adelaide and Signe, of all people! I didn't know you actually shopped at the real mall. I thought 'The Land of Mall Returns' was your favourite haunt. What are you here for?"

Oh great. Just what I don't need. I thought I was cranky before. The voice that dunked a thousand donuts belongs to my ex-best friend Lindsay Dixon. She is not exactly a person that I feel like seeing this very second.

"Shut-up Lindsay. Just because you work at Make-Up World doesn't mean that you are the goddess of good taste. What are you doing at the fountain anyway? Don't you have to trowel some concealer onto someone's face or something?" I was going to add, "So they will look just like you," but for once, I held back.

Lindsay and I used to be best friends all through grade school. We did everything together. We walked to school together, had lunch together, had haircuts together, everything. And so did our parents. Until this summer. Our friendship came to an abrupt end after our families spent July together out at Grand Beach. Her parents told her it was the worst month they had ever spent in their lives and how did my parents think that hanging around in a cottage drinking party drinks all day and night starting with Bloody Mary's first thing in the morning was a great time when there was sailing or water skiing or hiking or anything else but drinking to do. They also decided that Lindsay was going to be unduly influenced by me and my parents so they said -- "See you later -- Much" to me and my family within minutes of us pulling into our respective

25

driveways. The whole thing really hurt. You would think that maybe Lindsay's parents, who I honestly thought were like my own parents only sober and nice, would do or say something to me or Cliff or Dee but… I guess they didn't want to get involved or whatever. It has been a very quiet and lonely couple of months.

My father's explanation for why he never saw Bob any more was that he was a genuine milk-toast and could douse any fun with the giant wet blanket of his personality. Rationalize, rationalize. Anyway, my mom was really hurt by the whole fiasco because she felt like Dottie was the classiest friend she ever had and now she was gone. Not to mention that she had to see Dottie every Tuesday at the Women's Committee of the Ballet and everyone there had heard about our summer adventure. Hmm. It just occurred to me why my mom is having a difficult time making eye contact these days. The whole thing bugs me too but I haven't let on just how much I know about what Lindsay's parents said and all to my mom. She seems a little susceptible to the 26 ounce flu and criticism these days. It is bad enough I give her grief about my own weird stuff let alone her snotty friends. All the summer crap rained down on me from the mouth of Princess Lindsay. She knows how to get to me. I'm sure glad that Sigge has filled in the friend gap. She's like spa music, she's there and not there. Somehow that is really comforting right now.

I am jolted out of my feeling sorry for my situation moment by the annoying sound of Lindsay's voice.

"You know Sig--Knee, I am truly surprised that your parents actually let you hang around with addled Adelaide. She has a rather questionable heritage, an addictive gene pool. Heaven knows what type of people you will be introduced to. Be careful now."

Lindsay really knows how to get me good. We used to practice being mean. We would think of the worst thing you could do or say to someone but we'd never really say the stuff. Until now obviously. All our practice seems to have paid off for her somehow.

"Lindsay, you don't have to warn me about Addie. Remember I am the sister of Bernerd the Brain-dead, as I have heard you say. I apparently have my own questionable heritage. Nothing Addie or her parents can do can compare with my own personal hell living with the navel lint king. C'mon Addie." Sigge grabs the sleeve of my old used to be black sweatshirt and pulls me towards Grimson's. Save # 2.

"Bernerd is really cute though Sigge. That kind of hell is worth it!" Lindsay says almost swooning.

"You are sick, Lindsay, he's my brother." And with that, Sigge tosses a penny over her shoulder into the fountain and we split.

"Major cow." I growl.

"True Addie. Very true. But enough time wasted. Let's get to Grimson's before all of the good stuff is gone!" Sigge pleads.

"Let's not go to Grimson's. Let's go there," as I point to a very large and very pink neon sign that spells out RIO. "Let's go to Rio. They have very smooth stuff and if I walk in the door with a huge bag from there Slick will be furious. He'll launch himself off his chair and into a speech about his hard-earned and how Grimson's puts the booze on our table and he'll say oops Freudian slip I meant food, and I'll say easy mistake there are two O's in both words, an I'll have some wicked fun at his expense, twice."

"Okay Addie, you're the driver."

"Sigge, say that again."

"Okay Addie, you're the driver."

"Sig, you are a genius. That's starting to sound like a great idea. Let's get some seriously cool car driving and dating clothes. Sigge let's start our shopping engines."

5

At exactly nine-thirty-one my mom pulls into the passenger pick - up place. Sigge and I are waiting with our arms filled with lots of bags from RIO. The bags are unmistakably not from Grimson's; see through plastic pink and purple psychedelic moons crunch and crinkle. The crackle of transformation is in my sweaty little hands. Cool. Very cool.

I know exactly what mom's reaction is going to be as I slide into the backseat of the car with all of my purchases.

"Addie," she'll say, "what will your father say when he sees all of those RIO bags?"

Sigge is content to sit in the front seat and cradle a tiny tube of glitter that she bought for a painting she's working on. What's really cool about Sigge is she doesn't seem the least bit jealous of me spending all sorts of money. I don't know if I could be so generous. I'd probably be thinking, "Geez, the least the selfish b-I-zitch could do is share!"

"My goodness Adelaide, you certainly were able to put a dent in that money your father gave you. Look at all the bags. And if I am not mistaken, not a one is from Grimson's. Adelaide, you know what is going to happen don't you? Your father will have more than a few words about where his money went. What exactly were you thinking? Adelaide? Adelaide? Can you hear me dear?"

It is such a complete bore being able to predict the future.

"Addie and I saw Lindsay at the mall tonight Mrs. Sinclair. Oh yeah, and Addie got loads of cool stuff. You'll love it all. None of it is even close to a shade of grey. And the bonus was most of it was on sale. That's why she spent so much at RIO. Grimson's was too expensive. I bought some turquoise glitter. We had a great time too. We sat at the fountain, drank hot chocolate. You know the regular mall stuff. Oh here we are already. Just drop me off at the end of the

31

driveway, Mrs. S. I'll see you tomorrow Addie. Thanks for the ride in the amazing new steed. Bye."

"She's good," I think to myself. Save #3.

Me and my mom can hear Sigge's goodbye over the slam of the car door. We watch to make sure that she gets into her house. As the front door opens warm orange light pools onto the front step and sucks Sig right in.

I wonder what drowning in warmth feels like.

"Adelaide, I just have to say that Signe is such a friendly girl. You have such a nice collection of friends. I am surprised that you never have them over to the house. You can have them over any time you know." Mom pauses as if something deep has occurred to her.

"So, uh, Signe mentioned that you two saw Lindsay at the mall. Is that right? How is she?"

Oh great. Another conversation that smells like dread.

"Lindsay is … a total bag. She got a job at the make-up place in the mall and she thinks she's Queen Shit of Shitland."

Ohmigawd, swearing in front of my mother, OHMIGAWD. This Lindsay thing is bugging me more than I thought.

"A -- de -- laide! Have you forgotten who you are talking to? My goodness!" Mom says as she shakes her head and pulls the car away from Sigg's house.

"Anyway, Lindsay is not a b-a-g as you put it dear. She is a very nice girl. She used to be your very best friend, for heaven's sake. Just because she has a job at Make-Up World doesn't mean you have to be rude about it. If it was me who had a friend that could do make-overs I would be down there every night. You girls could have such a good time playing with all that make-up and doing your hair all groovy. I remember when you and Lindsay were little and Dottie and I would take you girls to get pixie cuts together. You were so kee-ute, the two of you. I just can't understand what could be so bad that you aren't speaking to one another. Addie, why hasn't Lindsay been around lately? Does this have something to do with a boy?"

As my mom rambles on I can feel my face fill with hot lava. I know I am just about to explode because I can see red-hot stars and nothing else.

"Why hasn't Lindsay been around lately? A boy? You must be joking. You aren't serious are you? Don't you know? Don't you remember that fiasco that you and dad called a summer vacation? Of course you don't remember. What am I thinking? Lindsay is not allowed to see me let alone give me a make over. I can hear her now mother, "'Here Addie let me add a little red eyeliner around your eyes and how 'bout I draw a few gin-blossoms on your nose. There. Now you look like the rest of your family!'" I rant.

As my mom manoeuvres the car into the garage I know I heard her gasp as she rams the car into park. I know where her jugular is. Practice makes perfect. Lindsay is not the only one capable of scoring an emotional bull's eye. Or being capable of feeling so relieved and so bad at the same time. Glad I said what I said, finally. I think.

Maybe we can start telling the truth from now on.

6

Mom certainly didn't stick around to wait and see how much I enjoyed my tirade. She threw the car door open and jumped out as soon as she made our abrupt stop. I wanted to get into the house fast for two reasons but she beat me to it. I wanted to escape the mad mother face and the flying emotional shrapnel also I wanted to try on my new gear. And I just had to tell the truth about the Lindsay thing. Mom may not think that she has a problem but the rest of the civilized world seems to think she does except for maybe my Dad. What a weird bunch we are. We all pretend that there isn't a problem and we all hide in our rooms or where-ever. Anyway enough of this. I have been so low and black moody lately that Dad's gift of cash was just what I needed. New clothes, new attitude. New me. If I can change, and somewhat painlessly, maybe Mom can to. Maybe we all can.

I collect all the bags off of the backseat of the car and head into the house. As I come up the stairs from the garage I can see that Mom is sitting at the kitchen table smoking and drinking coffee that is left over from dinner. Her hand is shaking and she looks really tired. I sit down on the stairs and attempt to take off my boots. It's a major two-handed job getting these things off. That'll teach me for wearing work socks.

"Adelaide. Can I see you please? I'm in the kitchen." I knew this would happen. Oh well. I better suck it up and face the old proverbial music.

"I'll be right there. Just a second. My boot is stuck. Oomph. There. Hang-on. Okay. Here I am and before you say anything, I know, I know. That crack I made to you in the car was over the top. But geez mom, what gave you such a crazy idea in the first place? What exactly were you thinking? Lindsay could give me a makeover? Ohmigawd." I know I am wrong but I am on a roll. I can be such a jerk.

"Addie please. To tell you the truth, I really had to get away from you in there before I said something that will be thrown back in my face. You are extremely chippy these days so I protected myself."

I am not sure why but I cannot bring myself to say I am sorry. Hurting her feels good. I don't like myself right now. I've got to get out of this minute.

"A good defence, Mom is the best offence. Oh by the way, you should see what I bought tonight. Serious gear. Seriously, awesomely cute, gear. Let me go and try it on for you. I bet you will really like it. I avoided black completely. I'll be right...."

Mom broke in before my escape.

"Addie wait. Don't go yet. I'd like to have a little chat with you if you don't mind. I need to ask you something. About the Lindsay thing. I had no idea that her parents were involved in you guys not seeing one another. I just thought you two were taking a break. When did all of this happen?"

It's weird and true but mom has no idea about any of this.

"A couple of days after we got back from the beach. It's no biggie. Sigge's fun and we get along. Lindsay thinks she is such a big shot now anyway since she got the job at the mall. I can survive without her."

I keep thinking I have to get out of here. Those puppy dog eyes of my mom's are way too much to take.

"Can I go now? I really really want to try this stuff on. We can talk after I finish modeling. I'll even make you some of my extra-speciality hot chocolate. You shouldn't be drinking that nasty old coffee before you go to bed anyhow. We'll talk some more if you want. Next time you see me you'll be completely amazed at my transformation."

I stalk out of the kitchen, sucking in my cheeks for my most stunning super-model look ever.

I figure if I throw some humour into this situation maybe we will both lighten up.

I can hear my mom mutter under her breath as I drift up the stairs.

"Yes dear. Okay dear. I'd love it if you would dear. I can hardly wait dear."

I hear her say this kind of stuff after my dad makes suggestions too, and in the same half-hearted way. I'm not sure if she's trying to make me feel guilty or if she is just seriously bored. Whatever she means, it sure makes me feel sick and weird.

Like I said before my room is my favourite place in the whole house. It is my nest. It has all of my favourite colours and textures. Zebra stripes, red velvet drapes, my mom's vintage purple lava lamp. The only annoying thing about my room is the heat registers. They act like giant sound amplifiers. I can hear my dad breathing five rooms away. Right now I can hear my mom rattling around in the kitchen; she is obviously no longer sitting at the kitchen table. I hear the cupboard doors opening and closing, glasses being placed on the kitchen counter. I am supposed to be getting changed but I am preoccupied with the sounds of my mother's habit.

Her sighs and longing looks at the ceiling somehow make me feel responsible for what is about to happen. I can't seem to stop this emotional car ride. I always say, "Oh well, who cares, it's her problem." And you know I always act like nothing matters and I'm a major brat, but it's getting harder and harder to ignore her behaviour. Someone has got to give in this show-down and I sure don't want it to be me. I'm Addie, cool, coy, removed. Untouchable. *Yeah, sure. I wish.*

I can hear my Dad come into the kitchen. I am going to try and ignore what I am about to hear. I pile my stuffed animals in front of the register and get down to the business of my personal transformation while my mom is transforming herself in … I have got to stop thinking about this. Once I am

39

done changing I will go downstairs, make some hot chocolate, apologize, chat and have a good, guiltless sleep. Yeah. And we'll both forget just how lippy I can be. Perfect plan. Now, I'll just slip into this orange and pink t-shirt and these new hippie flare green jeans and wow the awaiting masses.

As I am on the way out of my bedroom door I catch a glimpse of myself in the mirror. Cool. Acceptable. Different than yesterday. Maybe I will try out for the school production tomorrow and tomorrow and tomorrow. I will become a whole new person, a character in a play, that is amazing and confident, that can drive, that has a regular sober family, and is really rather nice.

****

It hasn't always been this way you know. My mom used to work. At Grimson's actually. That's where she and my dad met. She was one of the window designers. But there was this time when she was doing a particularly difficult design, hanging a chandelier thirty feet in the air, and she fell off a ladder and herniated a disk in her back or something. She's never been the same. She had a couple of back operations but she was still in a lot of pain even when she took her painkillers and that's when the drinking got worse. She says the liquor helps the pain medication work. But that was two years ago. Things have gotten way out of hand recently. She really must have loved her job. She really must be in pain. She really lost a lot.

"Good morning to you! Good morning to you! We're all in our places with bright shiny faces. Good Morning to you. Good Morning to you!" My mom is buzzing around my room, dusting my blinds as she opens them.

I can hear her singing the song that she used to sing to me in the mornings when I was little. It's wafting in and out of my consciousness like the smell of fabric softener and the comforting whirr of the clothes dryer. I feel warm and hugged. A delicious feeling, one that I haven't felt for what seems like forever. I don't want to open my eyes. This comfort feels too good, so it can't be real.

"Come on sleepy-head. Rise and shine Addie my love. It's Friday, your favourite school day. Up and at 'em sweetheart."

I recognize the voice as that of my mother, but it seems weirdly out of place. I pull the covers over my head and open my eyes to the pink fuzzy haze of my thermal blanket. I peek to make sure that I am not the incredible shrinking girl and that my legs are still as long as yesterday and that I am not in Teletubby flannel jammies. No. Good. Red and purple plaid boxers and my glow in the dark "Yeah Right" t-shirt. But none of this explains the cheerful sounding mother voice standing beside my bed. In a sunbeam, in the actual, real-deal morning. After witnessing my performance of last night I figured she wouldn't be seen until noon at least. And now she is singing in my room in daylight. Who knows? Maybe she took what I said in the car and the kitchen to heart. I won't hold my breath though. I'm too paranoid these days to be too hopeful.

"Okay, okay, mom. Ten minutes and I'll be up." I say from under my blankets.

And with that, as if in a poof of silver sparkles and tinkling bells, she disappears on a static-filled orange-shag cloud, still humming.

Moving out of my cosy sunbeam cloud of dust particles is going to be difficult. But, there is something unusual about the day so far, and I do have a whole bunch of new clothes to spring on the world -- so -- what the heck.

****

"Hey Mom? Sup? You're awake bright and early this morning." I say as I slide into the kitchen from the hall.

At the kitchen table, mom is sitting with a cup of fresh coffee and a smile. She is wearing an orange and white gingham dress with a giant white collar. Despite this, she looks good, even healthy. A newspaper sits open in front of her and an ad for Armond's Hair Saloon is circled.

"Adelaide, I feel so good this morning. Your father gave me a little of his raise too and I am so excited. I made an appointment with Armond."

"Armand? The Dixon's pool guy? Mom!"

"Oh for heaven's sake Addie. You and your father have the same sick sense of humour. No, not Armand the pool man, Armond the hairdresser. I don't think that is really his name but he does everyone's hair that matters, and I got myself an appointment this morning."

I shrug, "It's hard to imagine this town having two Armonds. Weird. Anyway mom, are you okay? You seem different this morning."

"Of course, silly. I'm sorry about last night. If I had known about Lindsay I uh well wouldn't have been so insensitive about the make-up thing and all. Sometimes I don't pay as much attention as I should. By the way, that outfit is smashing. Both of us look good in orange."

For some strange reason this overwhelming urge to hug my Mom just about strangles me. There she was chatting away as if, as if this is a new beginning or something. The whole moment felt so pathetic but so necessary.

I wonder when I stopped hugging her 'cause the next thing I know she is pushing me to the front door like she did in the first grade when all I wanted to do was hug her and smell the warm sugar coffee of her skirt. It's like I didn't want to let her go ever, that I could be forever safe and sweet. And now, again, I feel that, that I could bounce from here to the moon, the cool dark blue side. The old sweet me again, totally new though, totally cool and only a little blue.

8

The warm fuzzy feeling must have propelled me to Sigge's house. I don't even remember how I got there, just that I remember humming Blue Moon and admiring the new-look me in each and every puddle I jumped. When I got to Sig's door I knock like I mean it. And it isn't too long before Sigge opens the etched glass door and whistles shrilly in my direction.

"Oh Addie!" she gasps when she finds her voice. "I never realized how amazing you look in colour! Bernerd, look! It's Addie! Ohmigawd! You're tangerine! It's beautiful -- I mean, you're beautiful! Isn't she Bernerd?"

There goes Sigge's enthusiasm again. This time though it's not so annoying. It feels nice being admired. Who know I would get this kind of attention just by changing my clothes. First my Mom, now Sig. Awesome.

"C'mon Addie, let's get to school. Let's show you off. Wait 'til Lindsay sees you. She'll be sooooooo jealous!"

As Sigge closes the door behind us, I catch a glimpse of Bernerd watching us leave. I am not too sure but I think he might even have been smiling. "So Sigge, really, do I look okay? Is this outfit a little too, too?" I ask, my self-consciousness rearing its head.

"Ad, listen -- I haven't seen you look this good or even this happy in a very long time. So, yes you look okay. More than okay, better even. Okay?" said Sig.

"Okay. I'll let it go. It's just so strange being a Technicolor moment. I am so not used to it." I said.

"No biggie. But did you get that English homework done? Paraphrasing that Shakespearean sonnet was a nightmare. I don't know who Ms. Ostrowski thinks we are, but learn-ed scholars we're not. Geez. If she asked us to build a scale model of the Globe theatre maybe, but understand this King Lear stuff, ooboy, no way."

"Yikes, Sig. Yet another assignment not done. I may be looking good today but that won't save my sorry butt. Ms. O. is a major pain when it comes to late assignments. I'll just cut class and meet my mom at Armond's. She's getting all dolled-up today 'because my Dad cut her in on some of his raise too. You can think of a creative reason for my absence I'm sure. Call me later and we will plan an evening of videos and dill pickle chips and popcorn. See ya." With that I spun around and headed back home. It's about time I spent some quality time with my mom. After last night anyway.

****

It's an amazing feeling you get when the sun shines warm and clean on your back. It's almost as if you have your own personal power pack strapped on. I wonder if the sun gets tired of its own sunny disposition sometimes, like Sigge. Today though I like it. Nothing is going to take this warm fuzzy away if I can help it. Not even the knowledge that my English mark is slipping into the toilet. Right now I don't care about anything except change. And right now I don't care about anything except that I can smell the scent of the chocolate cosmos daisies in the Dixon's garden right here and I have a serious desire for a steaming hot café mocha. MMMMMM. I'll stop and pick up three of them. One for me, one for mom and one for Armond, just to be nice.

One of the good things about living in Silverwoods is that everything is close to everything else. One of the really annoying things about living in Silverwoods is that everything is close to everything else. Getting to Armond's is easy. It's just four blocks and a major thoroughfare from our house, and right next door to the salon is Brewster's Coffee Coop. When I am feeling good, living here is cool, but when I am feeling less than perfect, it sucks, big time. You can't run or hide. Everyone knows your business, you know, like the "Lindsay and the Lake" fiasco.

But enough of that.

My mom seems to be on track I think, I feel it's true, this time. Both of us will be "lookin' stylin'" to quote Grimson's catalogue and my father. This is going to be one cool skipping school kind of day.

Brewster's is cool. When I walk in it smells so warm and inviting. Chocolate cinnamon coffee cake is their specialty and they make the best mochas. Mom rarely treats herself well, so this will be a great day for her. Coffee from me, new "do" from Armond, approving nods from Daddy-o. Fortunately for me it's nine-thirty in the morning and there shouldn't be any teachers in here. I can scoot right in, get my coffees, and bop on in next door to see the new mom. I hope she's not too choked that I ditched school but it is for her own good. If we are together how could anything possibly go wrong?

Armed with the mochas I moon-walk bottom first through the salon door. At first Mom doesn't notice me, but I sure notice her!

"Ohmigawd Mom. How could you let Armond talk you into this?" I squealed. I winked at Armond so that Mom couldn't see. She looked great. Short little bob and cute little bangs. Youngish and red.

"What, What? Addie what are you doing here first of all and second, what do you mean? What is the matter with me? Don't I look all right? Oh my goodness, your father is going to have a fit isn't he? Armond how can I have let you talk me into this?" Mom wrings her hands and pulls at her hair.

"What dee-lish-e-us, Dee? How could I let you leave here not completely gorgeous. That IS what you mean, isn't it Adelaide? If it's not I'm going to have to dye that gorgeous hair of yours mouse brown. Oooooh you. That orange on both you and your mom is amazing. Few people do that colour justice. Awesome girls, just awesome." Armond gushes.

50

"Mom you look amazing. Getting rid of all that hair piled up on your head sure has taken a load off your shoulders. You look young and happy and so pretty. You really notice your eyes. I can hardly wait to hit the mall with you this afternoon and buy you a new outfit! Oh by the way guys I brought you some mochas. I was feeling extra-specially generous this morning."

"Thanks, sweet. What's the occasion Adelaide, that you want to get your mother all dolled up?" asks Armond.

Just as I was about to answer, I notice, two chairs down, Lindsay's mom, was plunked and draped, in anticipation of Armond's "hands of transformation."

"Yes Delores. Do tell. What exactly do you have planned for this evening? A cosy evening with Cliff ALONE, perhaps?" sneers Mrs. Dixon.

I couldn't bear to hear Dottie talk to my mom like that so in my very best polite but sickeningly sweet voice I said,

"Oh hi Mrs. Dixon! I just noticed you. Would you like a mocha? They're fresh from Brewster's and they're absolutely delicious. It's so nice to see you. It's been a long time."

I was speaking so fast that she didn't have time to say no to the coffee. She took it from my hand and immediately had a sip. She gulped it down and gave me a half-smile and a burpy thank-you just before Armond lit into her.

"Do you mean to tell me Dottie that you haven't invited Dee and Cliff to your soiree this evening? Frankly I am surprised at the two of you. You used to be so close. Dee, Dottie, get over whatever is bugging you. Dee is going to look so fantastic after her day spa treatment that it is a crying shame that it will only be witnessed by the staff. Dottie invite Dee and Cliff over right now. Think of it as advertising my business and I'll give you a free cut next month. I am so tired of these petty differences between my customers affecting my business I could just spit. Well Dot, I am waiting." Armond stopped back combing mom's hair with a great flourish.

I am sure that Armond is not the only gay guy is Silverwoods but he's the most obvious. I wish I could be more like him. He says and does whatever is on his mind. He's very strong and knows exactly how to get what he wants. Watching him manipulate my mom and Mrs. Dixon is like watching a conductor at the symphony.

"WELLL......" he said. "Dot?"

52

"All right. Dee would you and Cliff like to join us and the rest of the cul-de-sac at our wine and cheese this evening? Eightish. Gawd. I'll do anything for a free hair cut it seems. Especially for what you are charging these days, Armond. Are you happy now? Can you finish her and get on with Me? Armond if you were not such a master I would never have agreed to this. You obviously have no idea....."

"Here. Drink this." Armond says to Mrs. Dixon as he places the straw from the mocha cup into her mouth with precision. "It's soooo good. It takes away the bitchies."

You have to hand it to Armond. He is one pretty smooth and insightful guy. Not only that, he was able to do what I have wanted to do for Mom and Dot for the past two months, in seconds. He is a true master. Maybe I should let him have a go at my hair too. But first things first. My mom needs a rockin' outfit for tonight. This is so exciting. What an eventful day this has been so far and it's not even noon yet!

9

"Make this worth my while!" Bernerd yells into the phone.

"Hasn't anyone won that stupid contest yet Bernerd? Don't your friends think you're kind of geeky for saying that every time you answer the phone? I mean really, Bernerd. Do you actually think KZAM has you on their 'Nerds with no life' list? What am I thinking? Of course they do! Good luck Bern. They'll be calling you any day now! Can I speak to Sigge please?"

"Thanks Addie. For the luck. Yeah she's here. Just a sec." Bernerd says, politely.

Weird. No sarcasm.

"Hello Addie. You must be the luckiest person in the whole school, I swear. Ms. O wasn't even there today and the substitute gave us an extension on the paraphrase assignment so Ostrowski will never know you didn't have it done. I finished it, with some help from Bernerd, so you can borrow it for Monday if you want."

"Thanks Sig, I'll take you up on that. But I have to tell you what happened today. You won't believe it. Guess where Dee and Cliff are going this evening?"

"Your kitchen?" Sig sighed. Sigge is way more perceptive than I give her credit for.

"No, no, no. You are going to be amazed at the miracle that was performed by Armond today."

"The Dixon's pool guy? What could he possibly do that is miraculous? Except maybe notice me and ask me and you out for a glorious evening of fiery burritos and sangria?" There she goes visualizing again.

"Enough. No. Not that Armand. ArmOnd the hair guy. The do-boy to the neighbourhood socialites and suddenly my mother. He did my mom today…"

"Addie you are not serious. Are you okay? Does your dad have any idea? Oh this is just awful Addie. How can you call this a miracle?" Sigge is talking faster and faster as she goes on.

"Sig. Her HAIR. He did her hair. Good grief. Anyway I went to see her and maybe take her shopping, which we eventually did, but in the meantime, Armond got Dee and Cliffie an invite to the Dixon's wine and cheese party tonight. Armond was amazing. I am so loving him right now. He just stood there and Dot was getting all blue in the face and her eyeballs almost exploded and my mom was looking like a such a babe and Dot almost puked when she actually invited them and OOOO Ooboy Sig -baby this is going to be one cool reconciliation."

There was a definite long pause at the other end of the phone, and I could feel a definite sub-zero breeze on my cheek.

"Reconciliation? For whom exactly?" wondered Sig.

She is not jealous is she?

"Lindsay's and my parents, of course. My mom just hasn't been herself since Dot and Bob treated her so badly. You should have seen my mom this aft. It was like when I was a little kid and we'd go for lunch at Grimson's Grille. She was giggling and smiling and it was like it didn't matter that I had cut school. We got her this way cool outfit. She let me pick it out and everything. Black patent mini-skirt and an Orange ruffley blouse. I can hardly wait for tonight. Mrs. Dixon invited me and you to go over too because Lindsay is allowed to have a few friends over too. I don't know how Lindsay will react when we show up, but hey, her mother invited us, under hair-do duress of course, but an invite is and invite, right?"

"I guess," Sig said. "But I can't believe that you actually want to go over there. I thought we were going to hang-out and watch videos and eat popcorn and stuff. This feels pretty weird to me, Addie. Are you sure that you really want to go?"

"Yeah. I'm sure. I've got a whole bunch of swell new clothes to show off and what better place than at a party, even if it is at Lindsay's."

"Addie, I don't want to go. Something doesn't feel right. I'll watch a couple of movies with Bernerd I guess and maybe finish my painting."

It is weird and even though Sigg's right and it does seem strange and bizarre to be going to the Dixon's, someway, somehow, it feels like I just have to go.

"Okay Sig, but remember, there is always the chance that Armond the pool guy will be there. You don't want to miss him now do you?" I said trying to entice her.

"Nice try Addie, but nuh-uh. Not this time."

"Okay. I'll call you tomorrow, with all the dirt." I say, hoping there wouldn't be any.

When I hang up the phone I have a clenched fist for a stomach. Sig has never said no to fun before. I wonder what is on her mind.

10

From my room I hear the clink of ice on crystal through the heat registers. Shivers run down my back like an electric current. Nerves I guess. I can tell a celebration of a sort is going to happen in the kitchen. When my mom told my dad about the party this evening he immediately dove into his closet for his version of an outfit. He must be ready to go because the whole house has been fumigated with his "Indulge" after-shave. No rats or roaches will survive this stuff. Anyway I am as excited as my parents are to go to the Dixon's. It's been two months and it feels that the time is right for me and Lindsay to be friends again. It's not me who is the troubled one. Until Mrs. Dixon invited us over this afternoon, I had no idea just how much I had actually missed them all. I know that I've been grinding my teeth and having fists for a stomach every time I think of Lindsay. Being angry is such a waste of good tooth and time. I can practice being mean but I can't seem to get over being able to feel. Maybe all of us can be friends again. As long as my mom behaves herself tonight then maybe the Dixon's will trust us again. I wish Dad would pour her a "just cranberry juice" cocktail.

Anyhow, I'm just about ready to make my entrance into the kitchen and dazzle mom and dad. Another new outfit is going to make its debut. A little turquoise mohair mini-dress and pink fake suede thigh high boots. I am a complete vision.

I hear my father giggling over some bad joke he played on one of his co-workers and my mom asking if dad really, really like her new hair or if he was just humouring her. I wish she had his confidence.

I open the door of my room so fast and with such force that I make my own mini-hurricane. The breeze messes my hair and I look even better. I am so pumped and excited that I take the steps to the kitchen two at a time. I jump onto the black and white checkerboard tile floor, shake the house, and land with a giant smile and a question on my fuchsia lip-sticked lips.

"So fellow cul-de-sac dwellers when do we leave for the cheesy whiners party?" I ask breathlessly.

"Just as soon as your mother and I have finished our toddies," dad says as he swallows the last of his drink. The glass he is drinking from is made of cut crystal and it catches the light from the fixture in the ceiling. Rainbow sparkles cover his face and he looks good and festive. Until I catch a glimpse of the rest of him. I am not sure what exactly the message is that he thinks he is sending with this latest outfit, but I think it might be "help me find the vicious criminals who stole my real clothes!" Here he is displaying himself in an ochre velour body suit with a zipper from neck to navel. How can a guy who dresses like this work for a men's clothing store in a position of power? How completely blind is he? At least he isn't wearing the giant zodiac medallion of his youth that he usually drags out for festive occasions. Oh well, I will try to ignore this nasty fashion mistake and have fun tonight. I look at my mom and she is looking as cute as can be. She is wearing the new outfit we picked out this afternoon and some funky dangly earrings. I am happy she is looking so good and healthy. I always kind of survey her and try to figure out if she will have a little "episode." And so far so good.

My dad pours another crantini for himself and mom. I am definitely feeling like I want to shout at him and tell him to knock it off, that she'll be a basket-case before we even get to the Dixon's, but I hold back. I want to have a good time. I don't want a shouting match before we go. I want to be friends with the Dixon's again. I really hate feeling like this, like I have to be in charge and take control. I want to be the ridiculous one. They're the adults. They are supposed to know what they are doing.

"This will cure any bladder infection that's lurking in your system," Dad declares. "Bottoms up!" This just breaks him up and he repeats his bad pun,

"Bottoms up. Geez I crack myself up. So Dee, shake your hollow leg and let's get a move on to the Dixon's. It has been too long since we have heard any of Bob's hula songs on the ukulele that I am chomping at the bit to get there, just like Addie. Let's go, go, go Delicious Delores."

Mom smiles a half smile and gulps down the rest of her chilli pepper red elixir. Cranberry juice is an amazing color. It leaves a burgundy outline around Mom's mouth. Not a moustache exactly, something a little more sinister. It reminds me of those bag ladies that overdo their ruby red lipstick not quite on their lips. Right this second all the hairs on the back of my arms stand straight on end and I can hear Sigge's voice saying,

"Something doesn't feel quite right, Addie."

It seems that at this second she is right. I am feeling more than a bit nervous. I wish Sigge would come with me. Sorta. I need a friend and I just can't count on Lindsay.

Sometimes arriving fashionably late, is the coolest thing you can do, according to daddy dearest. But, he seems to have forgotten that it's THE worst thing if you are fifteen and three-quarters years old and in change mode. Absolutely positively the worst, considering that Lindsay and our old pals aren't expecting me and that when I walk down the stairs into the tiki-torch bamboo palace, ooboy, all eyes will be on me. But if I am serious about going to try out for the fall production at school, I better get used to being gawked at, so I'll try out my ultra-cool new transformed self in the next thirty seconds and hope to survive the surveillance.

As we approach the Dixon's front door, Frank Sinatra doing it his way, laughter, and the clanking of dishes, greet us through the screen.

"Cliff! Dee! Addie! Look at all of you. It has been too long. Get in here would j'ya!" chirps Mr. Dixon. "Dot look who has arrived! A little late mind you, but you haven't missed a thing! Dot, Dot, more guests have arrived. I wonder where that Dot is hiding. Don't just stand there Cliff, c'mon in anyway. You know everyone, make yourselves at home. Addie, dear, look at you! You look so, so bright and cheery. I am sure Lindsay will be surprised to see you. All the kids are downstairs. Go on down. Have some fun." Mr Dixon flaps and waves me toward the stairs as if he is doing some wacky tribal dance. He looks as nervous as I feel.

A hot and clammy hand pushes on my back. I know it's clammy because it sticks to the hair of my mohair dress. I imagine that it leaves an outline complete with manicure.

"Addie! Are your feet nailed to the floor dear? Mr. Dixon invited you to go downstairs with the rest of the kids. Off you go now. See you later." my mom says as she peels her hand off of my back. "You remember where to go."

She sounds very confident and cool, as if she had just been here yesterday or something, like she hadn't had to have her hairdresser beg for an invitation. Like Mr. Dixon looked like he was actually happy to see us and not just because he hadn't taken his thyroid medication. Maybe coming here isn't such a great idea. Maybe if I am really quiet about it I can sneak out of the backdoor before Lindsay even knows that I am here. I wonder if anyone can see my heart beating in my throat. Ohmigawd. I think my knees are on backwards.

"Yeah. Sure I do, through the kitchen and down the stairs…." I say hardly above a whisper. I waver on my suddenly awkward boots and lunge forward toward the kitchen.

"Addie you shouldn't have had that last drink before we left the house, kiddo. Hah! Geez I kill myself." my dad guffaws. "So Bob, how have ya been?" he continues and drapes his bell-shaped sleeves across Mr. Dixon's shoulders. I don't want to stick around to hear the rest of that scary conversation. Yikes. I pull myself together, will my knees to bend in the right direction, and wobble toward the back stairs. I can hear party noise going on, soda cans opening and arguments about music.

I hold my breath, and take step one of my descent. This isn't too bad. Okay now for the rest of them. There may be only thirteen steps but ooboy this feels like forever. Six steps down I realize that a deathly quiet has hit the basement. The sound of my feet and my heart coming down the stairs at the same time must have terrified everyone. Lindsay looks as if she's about to swallow her tongue. Erica, Lindsay's cousin, is whomping her on the back. The urge to laugh and smile like and idiot hits me, and I do both.

"Lindsay, HI-I-I-I!" I say, sweet and clear amid a breathy giggle, "I guess your mom forgot to tell you I was coming."

The only color left on Lindsay's face was "Shame on You" blush. I feel a little guilty and whole lot powerful to know I could shake her world.

"I thought you said she never wore anything but black and was one of those weird vintage metal lunch-box Goth girls," I hear Erica say to Lindsay's very pale face.

"She did and she was until an hour ago apparently," snapped Lindsay. "I've got to get myself some ice-water."

To replenish your veins? I think to myself. I should have said that out loud but hey, it's her house and her party and I am a guest and......Ohmigawd....Jason Keble....He is smiling at me and he's coming over here and what if he expects me to talk or something? No problemo! New attitude, new Addie.

"Jason, I had no idea that you would be here. Did I see you working at the mall at Dog-Hotties? It seems that everyone is working at Parkland. When did you start there?"

"Uh, last March, at the end of basketball season. But enough about me Angela. Your name is Angela isn't it?" smiled Jason.

"It can be if that is easier for you to remember." I manage a smile.

"No really. What's your name? If you're lucky and you tell me I might give you a call, maybe give you a ride, you know what I am saying?" he taunts.

"Do you have your license already? I get mine in a month." I gush. "I can hardly wait. The freedom, the fun, the wind in my hair and tunes with heavy bass vibrating the windshield. Oh and it's Addie. Addie Sinclair." I stick out my hand. Jason takes it. "Now we are formally introduced." Jason seems to be having a hard time letting go of my hand. Lindsay is staring at him and me and our hands and is having a hard time letting her stare go!

"Are you going to tryout for Dracula this year Addie?" Erica asks me from across the room. "You would make an excellent Lucy to Bernerd Baxter's Dracula. You look just like

I imagine a Lucy to look. Your pale skin and your copper hair are exactly Lucy!" Erica walks over and wiggles her way between me and Jason. She is definitely not the cow Lindsay said she was.

So on and on I went. Jason just stood there, not even trying to escape and Erica and I talked until Lindsay couldn't take any more. I think I am driving her nuts with my new clothes and sudden charisma. I told Erica that Sigge was okay but she wasn't Lindsay and Lindsay and I used to have a lot of fun but things and friends change but I really did miss her and it was time that I too got a job at the mall.

"Hey did you guys hear that my dad of the ochre velour got a promotion. To reward himself he went and bought us a hot and sorta new car! I am so excited to get my license. Then I can drive around Silverwoods cruising' for burgers and boys like you, Jason, who might want to go for a ride or two..."

Here I am openly flirting with Jason Keble in front of Lindsay. She has had the biggest crush on him since second grade. But you know what? I don't even care. I am having the best time. This is so fun. Everything is okay. I am okay. Things with Lindsay will be okay. I can just feel it. Jason is smiling at me and occasionally touching my arm. According to the National Geographic channel that is a definite sign of attraction. That and hair tossing and flipping. Everyone, except Lindsay is standing around me. I feel like my old self, not the black phase self, but the cute, goofy kid self, that runs home and sleeps by the light of the silvery moon. The fake silvery moon no less, but all mine.

"Hey," I say, "What time is it? It must be twenty minutes before or twenty minutes after the hour. There is a definite lull in the conversation."

"Lucky us," I hear Lindsay mutter.

I get the feeling that having me here and being the center of attention really bugs Lindsay. If I had come here looking like usual, moping and chewing my hair, she'd be much happier. And I think she overheard Jason say he's dying to go for a ride with me sometime. If I am going to get her back as a friend I have got to get her alone and we have to talk for real. Not just snips and snipes. I will tell her that she will be the first to go driving with me, not Jason, not Sigge, that we will find ourselves in exotic locales like Portage la Prairie or Plum Coulee. That we will eat Fatboy burgers and Beady Eye ice cream goog specials. We will be rebels. Freedom's just another word for Adelaide Blanche Sinclair.

Getting her to talk to me tonight might be a challenge though. Every time I make eye contact with her, I feel a stabbing pain right through my head. She is not exactly receptive to this reconciliation deal it seems. Maybe she will be tomorrow, after the shock of having me crash her party and making googly eyes with Jason has worn off. Maybe if my mom and dad stay one step ahead of the cocktail demons and behave. Maybe if her mom says it is okay. Maybe.

"It's twenty after eleven," Erica volunteers. "Forty minutes until the witching hour. Let's get the Ouija Board out Lindsay! Let's see what kind of scariness we can conjure up. Someone go upstairs and see if you can find some candles."

"Okay. I'll go." I volunteer. "I think I remember where Dot keeps them."

Walking up the stairs, I know I am being watched, assessed. I was obviously way too paranoid about coming here this evening. I am having a good time. The punch is good; the company is warming up to me. Maybe I am not so weird after all.

When I get to the kitchen I realize that Dot has reorganized her world. Finding the candles is way more complicated than I thought it would be.

"I'll just go into the living room and ask Bob where they keep the candles," I think to myself. I don't want to

71

disturb Dot because I can hear her telling an Armond story to someone through the bathroom door down the hall.

"Excuse me, Mr. Dix....." I cut myself off before I am noticed. Mr. Dixon turns around and sees that it is me who has tapped him on the shoulder. He has a rather frightened look on his face and his eyebrows start doing a crazy fevered tarantella on his forehead. He flaps his arms and blocks me from going into the dining room. No one is talking and the CD player is stuck on a hair or something and is repeating I did it my way, way, way, way, way, way.... Time has slowed down and the voices I hear are warped and low-pitched. I feel as though I am swimming in honey. Everything is sickly sweet and every action is exaggerated and sappy and impossibly slow.

In the corner of the dining room up against the wall is my mother standing on her head. Not that demonstrating gymnastics at a party is a terrible thing but she is not wearing any underwear and there is a room full of people who will definitely recognize her at the grocery store the next time she emerges from the confines of our home. I wish that I could pull myself out of this scene but I just can't. I am sick to my stomach but I just need to know how this is going to play itself out. I back into the kitchen willing myself invisible. Mr Dixon is standing in the middle of the room slack-jawed in disbelief and my dad has a half-baked proud grin all over his face. They are a study in contrasts these two. The ochre jumpsuit thinks he has one, cool happening chick for a wife and Mr. Dixon thinks he has a depraved porno-queen for a neighbour. I, on the other hand am thinking, How will I get out of here alive and mentally intact? I have yet to be detected. Breathing is no longer an option.

I am not prepared for the next worst five minutes of my life.

"How about a big round of applause for Dee-dee Sinclair, gymnast extraordinaire," rallies my dad. He is not sure, it seems, why a hush has fallen over the room.

Mrs. Dixon appears through the doorway of the dining room. My mom hears her entrance. She rights herself and plants her feet firmly onto the Dixon's forest green carpet. My mom, MY MOM, FOR GOD'S SAKE starts shouting.

"Dot Dixon. Just who do you think you are you holier than thou hypocrite?" my mom rants.

"Dee. Please. Oh for heaven's sake Bob. I told you this would happen."

"How could you tell Lindsay that she was so much better than Addie and that she shouldn't be friends with her?" Mom is getting worked up.

Mrs. Dixon's mouth is moving like a goldfish. I imagine bubbles filled with expletives floating up in the air.

"Addie and Lindsay have been inseparable for all of their lives. What you did and shaid was juss mean. Mean, Mean, Mean. Dot is mean. You meanie you."

All I could hear was the words shaid and juss. She is slurring now, Ohmigawd. This sing-song taunting of Dot by my mother is nuts. Where is my dad? Why isn't he doing something? What other humiliation waits?

Jason and Lindsay burst into the room.

"Hey Addie, what are you doing? Where are the candles? We are all waiting for you." said Jason, expectantly.

Mr. Dixon's voice startles me.

"Lindsay you and your friends should go back downstairs. Now. Dee, he says firmly, please let this go. Why don't you go home, get a good night's rest and we will continue this conversation tomorrow. You are obviously very upset."

On the word upset, my mom slaps Mr. Dixon across the face. She lands a good one too. A handprint reddens his cheek as he loses his cool.

"That is it, Delores. Out. Take your bare bottomed self out of our house this minute. Sleep it off. And you wonder why, why we don't want Lindsay hanging out with Addie. For heaven's sake Cliff, take her home, get her some help. This time..."

My legs spring for the front door. I am a blue streak launching itself onto the front lawn. My brain is boiling.

I have got to get away from here. I have got to get away from here. I have to; I just have to get the hell away from here.

I am running as fast as my pink fake suede boots will
carry me. I've got to get into our house to get the rest of my
money. I will think about where I am going later. Through the
back door, up into the kitchen through the hall up the stairs to
my room. Grab my Zebra purse from the bed run down the
hall, jump down the stairs into the kitchen come to a dead stop.
Lying on top of the kitchen table in the blood-red shadow of an
unfinished tumbler of Crantini are the keys to the new 'mobile.
I pick up the keys and clutch them tightly in my fist. I am
surprised at how heavy they are. I can feel the edges sharp and
cold against the palm of my hand. Solid, real. I pick up the
glass, gulp a mouthful, and then smash the glass on the floor.
Red cranberry juice seeps into the front of my dress and burns

the back of my throat. I slam out of the front door and stop to listen on the step.

My parents are still nowhere in sight. They probably didn't even notice that I had seen that whole nasty scene. They probably think I am still in the basement at the Dixon's oblivious to my mother's hi-jinx. They have no clue. I can still hear bits and pieces of argument and music trilling into the night from the Dixon's house. The air is cool and crisp. A sliver of the moon skewers a cloud like an olive. I've got to get out of here.

****

The driver's door to the car is unlocked. I slide into the seat behind the wheel. I put the key into the ignition. I lurch forward as I search for reverse. I just can't seem to get it right. Okay. There. I'll drive really slowly and no one will suspect a thing. All right. Okay. Uh-huh. Not bad. I'm out of the driveway. I'll just drive around the block a couple of times before I hit the open road, just to get the hang of this thing. I've watched my mom manoeuvre our cars forever, drunk or otherwise. It can't be that difficult. Okay. This is not so bad. I'll drive to the intersection with the traffic light. I'll feel better if I can follow someone.

"This is not good, this is not right," I rhyme, quoting Dr. Seuss as I follow a red Volkswagen van with flower decals all over it into the parking lot of Mike's Market. My heart is beating wildly in my ears and my chest, a syncopated off-beat wild animal song. I have to talk to someone. I am clutching the steering wheel so tightly I can hardly pry my fingers open. I finally get the car into park, turn off the ignition, and breathe. Huge gulps of air aren't how I normally breathe but after tonight, hey, what's normal. I have got to talk to Sigge. I am gonna burst if I don't. I dig for quarters in my purse and come up empty. I have to actually go into the market and buy something. Why can't my parents have cell phones like the rest of the civilized world? I am not hungry and I'm not thirsty. But I need change. I am going to have to get out of the car. Okay here goes. I open the car door with purpose, as if I drive the thing everyday. I throw my left leg out and tentatively search for the pavement. Now that I feel like I'm on solid ground I slide the rest of myself out of the car and into the store. I sidle up to the counter where I ask I my most controlled voice,

"Can I have change for a twenty? A ten and a roll of quarters?"

The guy, Mike, behind the counter is such a moron. He says,

"No purchase, no change." So I say,

"Okay jerk. Gimme a package of cigarettes. Your choice." I am amazed at how calm and cool I sound. I notice the look on Mike's face as he hands me back my change. Normally he doesn't check ID. Eight year olds can buy cigars from him I bet. But he is looking me up and down with giant saucer eyes. I decide to vamoose really quickly so I don't have to answer any questions. I catch my reflection in the store door as I am leaving and realize what Mike is staring at. It looks like I have been shot or something. Giant red splotches of crantini freckle the front of my dress. I have got to talk to Sigge. Time is still in honey mode. It is moving so slowly. But everything inside of me is speeding fast. My pulse in my forehead, my breathing, my heart are buzzing and pounding a maniac dance beat. I have got to get to the pay phone.

Just as I am about to pick up the receiver of the phone, the driver of the red van leans out his window and yells as he is driving away,

"I wouldn't use that phone if I was you. It's covered in ketchup!"

I would probably be grossed out if this were any other day, but tonight I just need to make the call and I'll ignore the unsanitary conditions.

I drop the quarter into the pay phone and dial Sigge's number. The phone rings and rings and rings. I am nervous that her parents will pick up the phone and yell at me for calling so late. Five, six, seven rings.

"Make this worth my while." drawls Bernerd into the phone.

"Bernerd. It's me Addie. Is Sigge there? Can you get her for me please? I know it's late but I really need to talk to her. It's major serious."

"What's the matter Addie? Lindsay give you an involuntary make-over?" Bernerd sneers.

"Bernerd, please, puh-lease get Sigge. This is an emergency. I mean it this time."

"Addie. Sigge is not here. She's babysitting. What is the problem? Maybe I can help." He must have heard my words starting to bleed a little.

"Are you sure Sigge is not there? If you put her on right now I promise that I won't ever be a rude-mouth to you again, ever. This is a really major thing here Bern. Besides," I say as I take a huge deep breath, "how do I know I can trust you?"

80

I must be completely loopy if I am considering asking Bernerd for help.

"Because Addie, I, as you constantly imply, am a nerd with no life, so I live for your and my little sister's crises. So okay. What's the biiiiiiig problem?"

"Well I stole my parents' new car, I'm running away and I'm quitting school." I said, rushing and pushing all the words together. When I say all that really fast none of those things sound like such a big deal. Just a major earth shattering disaster, but not a big deal.

"Oh. Okay Addie. Let's slow this down. Where are you?" Bernerd asks in the most calmest, chocolate voice I have ever heard.

"I'mmmmm at MMMMMMMM," I am having trouble talking around all the pounding in my head.

"Addie breathe, tell me where you are, then stay put." Bernerd continues to talk. "I've needed an excuse to get out for a ride tonight anyway. Do Cheezdoodles and Cherry Coke sound as good to you as a midnight snack as they do to me? Where are you Addie? I'll come and get you," Bernerd continues. " As fast as a speeding vintage Vespa will carry me."

Breathing is so hard. I am gasping as if every breath is my last. My face is wet and it's not raining. I am yelling and repeating the words, "Mike's Market, Mike's Market," over and over and over.

****

The sound of the dial tone and whirr of Bernerd's scooter interrupt my breakdown. I am staring at my spattered pink boots as Bernerd gently takes the phone receiver from my hand and unsticks my hair from the clotted ketchup. He pulls a red and white bandanna from his back jeans pocket, carefully wipes my nose, instructs me to blow, then replaces his hand on my nose with my own. I can't look at him. The ground is easy. It won't ask questions or look at me as if I am completely pathetic. I am glad Bernerd is here though. His presence has a very calming effect.

"Addie, Addie. Could you look at me for a sec, please?" Bernerd cups his hand under my chin and speaks ultra-slowly. "I am going to go in and get those Cheezdoodles and Cherry Cokes. Stay here until I get back. I need you to carry the bag for me. Nod if you understand English." Bernerd half-way smiles as he goes into the market. He looks pretty good for so late at night, as far as I can tell from not looking at him too closely. I look at the back of his scooter and notice an extra helmet. It is shiny black with silver stars all over it. "That must be Sigge's," I thought to myself.

"Cool lid, huh?" smiles Bernerd as he hands me the bag full of treats.

"Is it Sigge's?" I ask.

"No, it's my mom's. She told me to bring it for you so if you decide to drive the car home tonight you will be somewhat protected."

"Bernerd, you're a jerk." I say, even though it is kinda funny.

"Addie, you must be feeling better. That's the first name you've called me in half an hour." Bernerd says as he hops onto the scooter. "Come on. Get on behind me. Put the bag on the seat between us, wrap your ever-loving' arms around me, and let's go girl."

"Where are we going Bernerd?" I ask.

"Back to my house to wait for KZAM to call." he says without a hint of sarcasm. "Because I think you need someone to talk to, okay, and I need to indulge in a few of these treats. Stuff your wig into the helmet and let's go. I'm peckish.

I don't argue. I'm too numb. The pounding in my temples has subsided and my breathing is almost regular, but my heart will never beat the same.

13

The yellow glow from the Baxter's front porch makes a halo around Bernerd's motorcycle helmet. Oh sure, I think to myself, Bernerd the angel. How predictably cliché is that? My thoughts are running in big giant shoes through my head. They are noisy and annoying. I have no idea what I am going to say to Bernerd. He has been so nice to come and get me and all but I can't let him know the truth about everything. It was Sigge I wanted to talk to not him. This is soooo embarrassing. I am covered in cranberry juice, ketchup and tears and I am sure I smell like trouble.

"Thanks for the ride Bernerd. I guess I'll take my leave from you now. Apologize to your parents for me for calling so late and say hey to Sigge for me when she gets home. I really gotta head out."

"Addie? You are going where exactly? And just exactly what happened? "

"Well Bernerd, you see, I found myself with all those people who really truly bore me and it was getting too much for me to bear. I got into an argument with my parents and I just have to get out of town. The idea of spending another eight months in that school with those people, with parents who could care less if I am around or not, just became really unappealing Bernerd. So, I just wanted to say Bye to Sigge before I hit the road." I am such a sucky liar and an even worse actress. I can hear this speech being delivered with a fake English accent as I am saying it. I am so lame!

"So let me get this straight Addie. Explain to me again why you need to get out of town tonight. You stole your parent's car because you say that you were completely bored by Lindsay's party and that if you have to spend the rest of your life in Silverwoods you will die. What exactly did you need to speak to Sigge about that was so urgent that you were the biggest drama queen on the phone? You drag me out of the popcorn comfort of my rec-room for what? For this really bad performance? I thought you were different Addie." he sighs and shakes his head.

86

"I am different Bernerd. You have no idea how different. But I have to go. I really am sorry."

Bernerd looks at me as if I have completely lost my mind. He wasn't buying into my boredom routine any more than I was. I don't blame him for being angry but it's the best I can do right now.

"Bernerd, did you really tell your parents that you were coming to get me?" I ask, not looking at him.

"Yup. I did." he nods. "But I feel kind of stupid now. It's not as if you really needed rescuing or anything. You just needed an audience. I am going to go in and let them know you are all right. Wait here. I'll walk you home in a couple of minutes."

"No Bernerd, it's okay. It's not that far. Anyway, I need some time to think. Sorry I bothered you. Bye." I hang my head, look at my boots and then aim myself home.

I kick a couple of stones into a storm drain and listen as they fall. I think I hear them hit the bottom. I'm not sure. Weird. Why couldn't I tell Bernerd the truth? He wanted to help me. Maybe I am more like my mother than I am willing to admit. She needs an audience, I seem to as well. She denies she has a problem, so did I, just now. Oh man. This is worse than I thought. I am a complete lying flake. But I don't know if going home is such a good idea either? There is going to be a lot of explaining to do. Like where the car is, why there is broken glass all over the floor. I am so angry at my mom. I am so angry that my dad didn't do anything. I am so angry that my one time adequate life is now a complete mess. I am so angry at myself for being so lame. I don't know how I am going to show my face at school on Monday. I hope Sigge will talk to me tomorrow. I have got to get to bed. I wish I hadn't dragged Bernerd into this. And when he tells Sigge what a complete goof I was tonight she will know that something is up. Then I will have to explain it all to her and then I will have to apologize to her parents. And the list goes on and on. What a complete disaster this evening has been. It started with such promise. I could have had both Lindsay and Sigge as friends. I could even have had a date or something with Jason Keble, but ooh boy, not now. I can hear it all now, in the hall, at school on Monday. Lindsay will say in her best snot-faced twang,

"Hey Adelaide. I didn't know you come from a long line of circus freaks."

Or my personal favourite will be when she asks me,

"So Addie, um, when did you mom start modelling lingerie? Or not?"

I am definitely going to transfer schools. What with skipping classes to spend time with my mom for the disaster party, and not doing my English homework and being completely humiliated in front of all the people that seem to matter at my school, I have no real reason to go back there. Well maybe to clean out my locker. I have a couple of Sigge's cool drawings that I want to save and I want to have something to remember her with, cause now even though her parents have been good so far about us being friends, after tonight, after Bernerd tells them the Addie drama-queen story, chances of us still being able to hang out together, will probably be non-existent. My thoughts are popping in my brain. They are electrically charged, static-y and painful. I have got to get some sleep.

There is no one home and for this I am thankful. I am not the least bit concerned about where "they" might be because right now I really don't care.

****

The hours after midnight are creepy in my house. The furnace wheezes dust and clanks its vent armour even more loudly than usual tonight. I constantly give myself the willies seeing shadows as I jump down the hall to the bathroom. I always think someone is sneaking up behind me. My heart stops and I can't breathe. I have to tell myself that it is my own shadow, it's just me, but I am still afraid. I never walk slowly around my house, when I am alone and it is dark. There are too many things to be afraid of, like abysmal decorating and poor fashion sense. Oh yeah, and the essence of drunken parents. I hope no one finds the time to bottle that heady scent.

I find myself in the safest room in the house. The bathroom. I lean against the door. I lock it and then pull out a drawer to act as a very dead bolt. I am gasping for air again. I feel like there is a circus elephant in a festive red collar with bells balancing on one foot on my chest. I lean over and run hot water into the tub until it is half full. If I run both the hot and cold water together our pathetic water tank runs out of the hot stuff. The things you learn about home maintenance. I add the right amount of cold water. I am the creator of the perfect Addie soup.

I am about to slip into the bath when I notice some facial tissues in the waste basket. They are covered in a series of fuchsia lipstick blottings from my mother. I guess she was experimenting with finding the perfect "how to shatter your daughter's life" colour. Every time I see tissues with lipstick on them I get so sad. Since I was little I used to imagine that the lipstick was blood. That the tissues were some kind of omen. That they were going to be the last artefacts of my mother left to me. That I was now an orphan. Geez, Bernerd

91

is right. I am and always have been a serious drama queen. Enough now Addie. It's bath time.

The water is the perfect temperature to soak tonight off of me. Actually a loofah would be much more expedient. I will remove all vestiges of my old skin that feels so tired. The new pink me that is just under the surface, will be released, now. The person that I thought I was tonight was just a pretender. Tomorrow and tomorrow and tomorrow. They'll see. They'll all see. The real me.

15

The sound of church bells calls me from my sleep. Then it's the sound of my alarm clock, and then I realize I am asleep in the bathtub and the church bells and the alarm clock are really the phone. There is no one that I want to talk to right now so it can ring all it wants. It's probably my parents. Let them worry. I will submerge myself until I can no longer hear it. The warmth of the water is so perfect. It is body temperature and I can't tell the difference between the water and my skin. When I come up for air the house is completely silent again. The phone has given up yelling. I notice a bruise on my wrist. I pick up my razor and very slowly and very intently shave each of my legs. No hair has escaped. I am smooth. I trace the outline of the bruise with the razor. It could be so easy to… Get out of the tub.

My bathrobe puts its arms around me and holds on tight. It is a very cheerful lime green chenille with red and pink cherries on it. It makes me run and dance to my room with feet of fury. It is warm and friendly and my current best friend.

I secure my room with a butter knife in the door jamb. It is my version of a lock. I pull out my black paper journal and a pink metallic milky pen and commit this day to paper.

> *Dear Stupid Diary:*
>
> *You won't believe the fantastic day I had. I went to a wicked party, doubled on a cute boy's scooter, and contemplated carving my wrists while I shaved my legs. Cool day huh? Later, much. Addie*

The phone is ringing again. I get the feeling if I don't answer it, it will ring all bloody night. I pick up the phone and,

"I'm home alright. You don't have to keep call…."

"Addie, Addie, it's me Sigge. What's going on? Can you talk?"

"Oh Sig -- Oh Sig--" I could feel myself starting to deflate. All I could say was Oh Sig, O Sig and then it all came rushing out.

"I am so sorry Sigge. I shouldn't have called you so late. Now I have gotten you in trouble and I told Bernerd all sorts of stupid lies about being bored and that nothing mattered and he's probably choked with me and your parents will never let us be friends and I have made such a mess of this whole night and I should have listened to you in the first place and we should have watched a video and Sigge I even thought how easy it could be to slit my wrists while I was shaving my legs and oh my gawd Sigge, what have I done? And the house is so creepy and it's late and my parents aren't home and I don't know where they are and I am so scared. What am I going to do now?"

"Addie, listen to me."

"Sigge, Siggeeeee." I know I am moaning but it feels kinda good.

"Adelaide. Ad-e-laide!" Suddenly it was Bernerd's voice yelling into the phone. He was raising his voice and pointing it at me.

"Addie. Sigge is coming over to your house right now. She will ring the doorbell twice so you know that it's her. You have got to come here tonight. Write a note to your parents. Tell them that you are here. Bring some extra clothes. Don't worry. We will figure something out. We don't want you staying by yourself okay. Sig is coming."

"Bernerd. I am only wearing a bathrobe."

"Save that for another time, Addie. For now let's just get you comfy and cozy."

"Bernerd. I didn't mean that."

"Oh. But a guy can hope can't he? See ya."

Just as he hangs up the phone our doorbell rings twice.

16

I stare stupidly at the floor as if I do not understand the meaning of a doorbell. It is ringing more insistently than usual. With stiff knees I robot walk to the door and open it. The street light is sitting on Sigge's shoulder. It flickers and winks its fake moon eye at me. I am distracted by the both of them and my enthusiasm is less than it usually is when I have visitors. I wonder if this is always how you feel when you steal a car and witness a potential black-out mother moment. I try my best.

"Sig, uh, Hi." I say in my best monotone. "What are you doing here at this time of night? Shouldn't you be babysitting? Oh I guess you are kinda, in a way. You don't have to stay you know. I'm alright. I am taking this drama stuff way too seriously these days."

"Addie, I am so worried about you. Bernerd told me about… that you called from Mike's Market and that you were a teensy bit upset. Can I come in? I feel silly standing here in the dark on the front doorstep? Oh Addie you're shivering. Let's get a blanket and wrap you up" Sigge said in her best mothering voice.

"Sig. I can't believe I got you involved in this mess. I'm just going to stay home. I'll be okay. I just need some sleep that's all. Sleep will help take the edge off. Seriously. I am fine." I am pleading with Sigge and I sound whiney. I wish my words would push her away.

"I don't think so Addie. Let's go into the kitchen and you can make me that special hot chocolate that you always brag about." She said. She is just like the doorbell, more insistent and sure than usual.

I look at her blankly. It's all I have right now.

"You know the stuff I'm talking about, Addie. The hot chocolate that you make for your mom."

"Sigge, I'll make you some hot chocolate, but you will have to promise me something."

"Sure Addie, what? You don't want me to reveal the secret ingredient right? No worries. Your secret is safe with me." Sigge smiles all innocent and friendly.

"I don't want to talk about IT, not tonight, not ever." The edge is still in my voice. I hope I don't sound too on the verge of tears.

"Sure, fine, whatever, Addie. I'm thirsty and cold. Make us a couple of warm drinks and let's get over to my place. But first let's get out of the doorway. Having this conversation here is not exactly cozy."

Sig is very sure of herself. She seems so strong at this very minute. I feel very small and tired and weak.

"Sig. I have to sit down." I grabbed the door handle and sat down on the floor. Sat is a dictionary term for the collapsing rag-doll action I just performed.

"Addie," Sigge sighed. "Let me help you into the kitchen. Come on my jelly friend. Let's get a solid piece of seventies furniture under you."

The street lamp went out decisively as Sigge slammed the front door with her foot. She got behind me and stuck her arms under my armpits, clasped her hands together and was dragging me to the kitchen when I caught sight of myself in the front closet mirror. Very not pretty. A limp lime chenille version of myself and I didn't do a damn thing about it. I just let poor Sig drag me and take care of me. It felt good and so selfish. I let her plop me into one of the chairs at the kitchen table and proceed to fuss about the kitchen.

"Okay coffee mugs, where does Dee hide you?" Sig hummed as she hunts through cupboards.

"Left cupboard over the sink." I mumble.

"Thanks Addie. Now what do I have to do?" she asks.

I don't really want to talk. I don't really want to tell her how to make stupid and really not so special hot chocolate. I don't really want to do a lot of things. But sometimes you do stuff that you never think you'll do. Like my bonehead move tonight. Go figure. I thought the driving thing was going to be fun and exciting not nerve wracking and sick-making. But ya know, even though I don't want to talk, Sigge makes it so easy. I guess that explains her middle name, Patience. She certainly is and has been with me. She makes me think and now, talk, even when I really don't want to.

"Okay Sig. Get out the cocoa and the mint flavouring. Right cupboard by the fridge. Get the milk out of the fridge. Get a pot from under the stove. Pour two mugs full of milk into the pot. Heat it up on low. You don't ever want to burn the milk. It tastes really yucky when that happens. Oh and Yeah. I forgot to tell you to put a couple of drops of vanilla along with the peppermint stuff. Put a couple of tablespoons of cocoa into each mug, enough sugar to make you happy, a couple of drops of milk, then stir it to make a pasty looking chocolatey goop. Pour the warm milk in it and voila groovy minty hot chocolate. Oh and can I have mine in the Peter Rabbit mug? It always makes me feel better."

"It's dirty and it is still in the sink, Addie. Sorry."

"It figures doesn't it, Sig. It just figures. Exactly when you need things the most they somehow, someway always let you down." Okay where did this outburst come from?

"It's just a mug, Addie." Sigge offered.

"It's way more than that, Sigge." Suddenly I am indignant. "I always drink out of that mug when this kind of stuff happens. It's the one thing that I can depend upon being there. It should be my mother's job, not the damn mug's. You even take care of me way better than she does these days. None of this is right Sig. I should be making hot chocolate for you. You should not be making it for hysterical, wobbly me. This completely sucks, Sig."

"I followed your instructions Addie. I am sorry it is not as good as you make it."

I think Sigge looks sad but there seems to be a twinkle in her eyes. How can she twinkle at a time like this? What is she thinking? I feel so sad. And all of a sudden here they are again. Tears. Tears and more tears leaking out of my eyes. I thought the bath had fixed all of this.

"Sigge, it, the cocoa, is great. But I am so not. I have to get out of here. You have to get out of here. I am in so much trouble Sig. I stole the car. I can't even drive and I stole the car."

"I know. Bernerd told me. What happened at Lindsay's Add? What could be so nasty to make you steal a car and put our joy-riding futures in jeopardy?"

"Dee, um, well Sig you have to…Oh never mind. I said I wasn't going to talk about this and I am not going to talk about this."

"So you think I can't keep a secret, Addie? Nice. I thought we were friends. I thought we could tell each other anything and everything. But I guess not. You don't trust me."

Apparently Sigge's patience is wearing a bit thin.

"It's not as if my mother's bare bottom is going to be a very well kept secret, Sig. That or the fact that she biffed Mr. Dixon upside his head and left a beauty mark in the shape of her hand on his cheek and that all of Lindsay's friends and relatives and all of the neighbours and last but not least Jason Keble were there to witness her performance! But if you want to try and keep it a secret be my guest. There. Now you know. That's what is so nasty. See. Now you can go home. NOW. If you are going to keep this a secret from anybody it should be your parents. They won't let you see me anymore you know if you tell them the truth. Just like Lindsay's parents."

Sigge didn't flinch or flicker. She listened with her head tilted to one side as if whatever I was filling her head with was going to dribble all the way in. She was going to catch every drop of my sordid story.

"Oh. That's what happened. I always wondered why you guys never hung out anymore. Mr. and Mrs. Dixon wouldn't let Lindsay be your friend. That's gotta hurt Addie. Why didn't you tell me? Don't worry about mes parents. They are pretty cool. Come on. Get dressed. Come to my place. Nobody will throw you out tonight. Tomorrow morning you may run out screaming from spending too much time with Bern but no one will throw as much as one little red hair out the door. You'll see. Mes casa, su casa." Sigge offered.

"I don't know. I feel really stupid and nauseous. Do you think a person can die of embarrassment?" I asked.

"Bernerd is my brother and I am not dead yet, so I think it is highly unlikely. Get dressed. Let's go. Forget about the hot chocolate. I will write a note to your parents to tell them where you are so they don't worry."

Sigge amazes me. She is such a good person and she is my friend.

"Would you also mind writing that the car and the keys are at Mike's Market in case they are wondering?" I asked.

"No problemo amigo! Now can I ask you a question?" Sigge pauses, "Am I not the most multilingual person you know Addie?"

"Sig," I pouted as I slouched out of the kitchen, "You are the only person I know who knows every language cliché imaginable. I will be dressed before you can say, 'a demain'."

"A demented to you too Addie," cackled Sigge in a dangerous sounding stage whisper, "a demented to you my wacky, wacky, friend. And, now that you have gotten the first part of the 'secret' out, let's get the REAL truth out of your mouth and into the open, once and for all."

I am not prepared for the greeting Sigge and I receive when we get to her house. It is 1:30 in the morning and you would have thought that it was seven. Every light in the house is on and I can hear the sound of a coffee maker freshly dripping in the kitchen. It smells like breakfast with a little turpentine thrown in for good measure. I can hear music playing somewhere in the house and it isn't Frank Sinatra or Dean Martin but the eighties band Orchestral Manoeuvres in the Dark. I recognize the song. It's called Enola Gay. I think that's fitting as my personal soundtrack.

As soon as Sigge opens the front door an orange puddle of light swallows us. It is the Baxter version of a transporter beam, just like on Star Trek I am painlessly and swiftly planted onto the round purple carpet inside their front door. I remember seeing this happen to Sigge before. Now I know what it feels like.

"Addie, it is so nice to see you dear." smiled Mrs. Baxter. "I'm glad Sigge was able to convince you to spend the night. Do you mind if I give you a hug?"

I shake my head and whisper, "No I don't mind." And with that she wraps her arms around me and squishes me like I won't break. I'm not sure if this is how she greets all of her guests but it was kinda nice. It's especially friendly seeing as how it is the middle of the night! Usually unexpected guests at almost two in the morning aren't greeted with many hugs unless they are long lost relatives not fugitives.

"Sigge, take Addie's jacket and hang it in the hall closet please. Addie come and sit with me in the living room. Can we get you a drink or something?" Mrs. Baxter is going out of her way to make me feel comfortable.

I shake my head to say no and proceed to walk into the living room. It is such a cool room. The walls are painted a charcoal grey and all of the furniture is purple velvet. There are lots of plants, palm trees and other tall things that are real and not plastic like the ones in my house. The closeness of the wall and bigness of the furniture in the room makes me feel totally small and really unworthy of being here.

"Uh Mrs. Baxter, I really shouldn't be here. Look at what time it is. I shouldn't be keeping you guys up like this. I 'm going to go." I say with as much conviction as I can muster. I try to spin on the burgundy leopard slippers Sig loaned me and bolt for the front door but Mrs. Baxter has anticipated this move because she is directly behind me, blocking my path.

"No, Miss Sinclair, you are not going anywhere. I would like you to sit down with me and have a talk. I know this isn't going to be easy but you will have to tolerate me for the next few minutes. As for keeping us up, it is no problem at all. I am working on some sketches and Mr. Baxter, Bern Sr. just got home from his shift at the group home. Bernerd is watching a Dracula marathon, prepping for the production, so, there you have it. We are all burning the midnight oil as they say."

"Oh," is the most insightful thing that I can think of to say. Mrs. Baxter and I both drop into respective corners of the couch and eyeball one another. She has an impish grin on her face and a twinkle in her clear grey marble eyes, just like the one I saw in Sigge's earlier. I must look scary bedecked as I am in pink flannel girl power pj's, damp red stringy hair and blue eyes staring into the headlights of her twinkle.

In another room I hear the phone ring and Mr. Baxter answering with a distant hello. Then I hear footsteps, whispers, then more footsteps.

"Addie, Bernerd told me about your phone call this evening. What happened darlin'? What scared you so badly?" Mrs. Baxter asks quietly and without any judgement that I can hear. Boy is this weird. It is the first time that any adult has ever asked me anything about my situation. The Dixon's are always so mean and opinioned and they just accuse me of stuff. They don't seem to care about me. Now, Sigge's mom, a lady that I hardly know, is asking me stuff I'm not sure that I want to share with a virtual stranger. But what is worse? Talking about this stuff or not talking about this stuff. Maybe she should be asking my dad questions. This is really uncomfortable.

The awkward silence is broken by the thumping sound of someone running down stairs.

"I'll be back in about five minutes, Mom!" shouts Bernerd as he rushes out of the front door.

These people are certainly busy for so late at night. I wonder if this activity explains Bernerd's obsession with Dracula. Now I am being ridiculous. No. Now I am beginning to feel normal. Earlier this evening was ridiculous, now is like it used to be, sorta.

"I wonder where he's going... No doubt it is important." Mrs. Baxter states. "Bernerd wouldn't run out for any reason. He is such a great person. You can trust him with your life."

Mrs. Baxter is definitely proud of her kids. Why does it seem that everything she is saying to me feels like a secret message? It's just like when you're listening to the radio and you are trying to figure out the meaning of life or something and a song comes on that answers your questions and tells you everything is going to be alright. Well, that is what Mrs. Baxter is like right now. The only problem is I don't seem to have very good reception tonight, because I am missing her meaning. Maybe if I pay closer attention I'll get it. I wiggle further into the corner of the couch and look as alert as I can. I wonder where Sigge has gone when I can hear a bath being run. I can smell bath bombs from the aromatherapy store. Calm is the scent she has chosen to unwind with this evening. They are the kind I bought for my mom's birthday. They obviously didn't work for her.

"I like the smell of those things don't you Addie?" smiles Mrs. Baxter as she takes a deep yoga-type breath. "They have such a calming effect on me after a night over the drafting table. Your mom used to do design didn't she, Adelaide?"

"Yeah, Mrs. Baxter, she was and by the way, this has been the weirdest night of my life." I launch into an impromptu speech since she mentioned my mother. "No doubt you are going to hear about it from Sigge and you've already heard some of it from Bernerd. I just don't know what to do. I am going to have to change schools because I am not going to be able to show my lame face around Silverwoods Secondary again because I will be the laughing stock of my whole grade. Lindsay Dixon will make my life at school a living hell as if my life at home isn't bad enough so essentially I have nowhere to go that is anywhere close to normal. Except maybe the moon, Mrs. Baxter. Maybe the moon will have me. The dark side that is."

At my last dramatic pronouncement the front door swings open and Bernerd flies in.

"Mission accomplished," he announces. "Moon unit retrieved and deposited and now good night. To sleep perchance to dream. Night Mom." "Oh and uh, Addie, make them sweet dreams ladies. See you in the morning."

"There is probably a very reasonable explanation for that so, go on Addie. Don't let the interruptions interrupt your train of thought. Don't get derailed."

There is her goofy twinkle again.

"Like okay, Mrs. Baxter, my mom has a problem, with alcohol and percodan. It's a painkiller she needed a few years ago when she hurt her back doing a design. My life ever since has been a strange bad movie. I thought things were getting better but ooboy, tonight. It is the icing on a really bad cake." I am blabbing but the words keep falling out of my mouth.

"Oh yes, Addie I remember hearing something about her fall but I didn't know about the 'problem' exactly. Sigge has had some suspicions though. What has your father done about this, Addie?"

Sigge has suspicions? I thought I was so careful.

"Nothing really. He likes to think of her as his party girl wife. They both drink too much, but she gets sloppy but he doesn't. He thinks she is funny and wild. She just can't function without a drink or remember whatever has gone on. When he goes to work, I pick up whatever pieces of our world that I can. The last two months have been the worst though. I have been able to cope pretty well till now. Now I don't know

111

what to do. I don't want to go home, I feel like I can't go to school, and now that I am going to have a police record well, cardboard box under the bridge here I come."

"Addie you certainly do have a flair for the dramatic, don't you. You know, I really appreciate you telling me. It couldn't have been easy for you. I had no idea that you were dealing with all of this by yourself. No wonder you were so frightened this evening. No wonder, no wonder. I know that this will seem like an easy fix and that I am not offering you any concrete solution at this time but why don't we both turn in and have those sweet dreams that Bernerd wished for us? We'll work on what you are going to do in the morning. I am sure you will come up with some kind of solution in your sleep. Your imagination is wonderful."

"I guess." I say with sarcasm dripping from the s.

I can't believe what just happened. I have never talked about this before and now I have to go to bed and not have it resolved. I feel cheated. I dump all of this on her and she didn't even fix it. She didn't even try. No wonder I have kept my mouth shut about it all for so long. No one cares. No one can help.

"Let me help you up, Addie. This couch likes to swallow newcomers. We found Uncle Al in there last week. He'd been in there for three days." Mrs. Baxter tries to joke.

I look at her blankly with snaky, slitted eyes.

"I am sorry dear. I can see you are in no mood for jokes. Give me your hand, please. I will pull, but you are going to have to give yourself a bit of a push up and out. Heave darlin'," she groans as she gently yanks me upwards.

"Ho," I grumble and follow Mrs. Baxter upstairs where I stumble my way to Sigge's room and an awaiting turned down bed.

I stare out the window in Sigge's room and pretend to
be asleep. The moon is hiding its face from me. It is
embarrassed too. I am so drained. I don't feel like talking
anymore tonight. I hear Sig come into the room and whisper
good night to me as she gets into her bed. She is sweet but not
so sweet that she kept her suspicions about my mom a big fat
secret from me. I can't believe her. She probably has told the
whole Baxter clan everything. No wonder they are being nice
to me. Just what I need. I am a major pity case. This is so
embarrassing. I feel like I am going to throw up. No wonder
the moon is hiding.

The rhythm of Sigge's breathing tells me that she has
hit real sleep. I sit up and wait to see if she is just trying to

fake me out. I certainly don't want to disturb the Beauty. She has had a way busy day with all this emotional hoo-haw and now me invading her room. Who knows what other kind of stunts she'll pull. I get the feeling that Sigge is way more complicated than I figure.

There is no way I can fall asleep. I will go downstairs to the rec-room and lull myself into a coma by watching a few infomercials. I really like the ones that have celebrity endorsements. Like as if Cher really waxes her own car. Anyway I will make like a ginger-cat and skulk down the stairs and try not to wake anyone up. The Baxter's might be pitying me but the last thing they need is an impromptu alarm clock rousing them from their hard earned zzzzzz's.

I wonder if my parents know where I am. I wonder if they care. I guess they have found Sigge's note by now. I kinda wish they would have come here screaming and pounding on the door and, you know, drag me home by my ear and ground me for life. That would make sense. Sorta. But being fifteen and a half is the worst. One minute you are perched on the edge of freedom with a bicycle and a Bart Simpson helmet the next you can taste the open road because you almost have your driver's license. You want to be all the things you wanted to be as a kid, able to fly, laugh, cry and giggle like a maniac whenever you want. You want to be as

115

wild as you can, adopt personalities that really aren't you and forget your manners. But you can't because all the things you want to do and be are being done to a frightening extreme by your mother. What? you say. My mother is behaving like a maniac. Yes, I say. More often these days, than not. It is hard to be a misbehaving teenager when you have got serious competition on the home front. It's hard to be a teenager period, when you have got to act like the mom. Why does philosophy happen in the middle of the night? I seem to be a better thinker in the dark.

So after skulking so quietly and stealthily to what I thought was going to be a deserted rec-room, it isn't.

"Nosferatu, is that you mumbling on the stairs? And just what exactly do you have against Cher anyway?" a disembodied Bernerd voice floats from beneath a comforter on the couch through the icy blue TV haze of the rec- room.

"Oh. Hi. Um, gee Bernerd. I figured you would have been asleep a long time ago. Sorry to disturb you. I'll go back upstairs." I said, embarrassed to have been caught mumbling about Cher and also to be hanging with Bernerd in my pyjamas.

"It's okay Addie. I need the company. This is one scary, creepy cat. Nosferatu makes you want to stay on the couch and forget about getting the cheese doodles. Do you ever wonder if the guys that play scary characters in movies have bad dreams? Come and sit on the couch. Not too close though. I don't want to get Addie cooties."

"Is that a shot, Bernerd? 'Cause if it is I can give you some really scary Addie material to regale your foes with. It's not as if you'd have friends." I blustered at him all puffed up and defensive.

"Whoa Adelaide. Back right off. Off the couch. Out of the room. You are one major piece of competition for the Dracula dudes. Go file you incisors darlin'. You only punctured half of my jugular. Ouch." Bernerd yelped.

What was I thinking? Here is this guy who rescued me from Mike's Market in the middle of the night and I can't even be civil to him. I am a MAJOR b-a-g.

"Bernerd. I am sooooooo sorry. I don't really bite, but I do seem to have developed a nasty bark quite recently, like now. I didn't mean to yap at you. Really. Can I stay if I promise not to speak?" I am grovelling.

"Look it's a Cher-mercial!" I point frantically at the television. "She is selling CheezSpray. I hope this is not her new fragrance line. Can you imagine getting to inhale that scent when the ladies who lunch walk by you in the mall reeking of that? Yuk. Cheddar on legs. Nasty." I keep talking even though I said I wouldn't. I figure if I say something witty he won't want to send me off to the nether regions of his house. I figure if I keep on talking I can segue into a thank-you for saving me speech and then when the sun comes up I can leave the house more gracefully than when I arrived.

"Addie you don't have to fill the silence with anything else but your breathing. Apology accepted but my guard is up. Just to let you know. You have had a gruesome night. I understand, but hey, don't take mine down too." Bernerd says deliberately.

These Baxter's are more assertive than I realize. Sigge, Bernerd, their mom and probably their dad too, for all I know. He is the only one I haven't talked to so far tonight. But considering how the rest of the evening has shaped up, I will be chatting with him soon no doubt.

"Bernerd. I would really like to say thank-you for picking me up tonight. It was nice that you would do that for me. I haven't been the most cordial of people to you and you picked me up anyway."

I am having a hard time looking him in the eyes. He has the same clear grey irises that his mom and sister have. The difference with his are that they are more like lasers than twinkle beams. He bores right through you when he looks at you and he is looking at me right now and remember earlier this evening when I was walking down the stairs at Lindsay's house and my heart was pounding so loudly in my throat and chest that I thought everyone in the basement could hear it? Well that is what is happening right now. I can't explain why exactly but thumpity, thump, thump, thump.

"And I have to say," I went on, "you have the most rockin' scooter I have ever seen or been on. It is amazing. When did you get it? What's it called again?" I chirp while looking at a spot on the wood panelling that approximates eye height.

"Vespa. Groovy, cool, totally sixties, original parts. That scooter -- m-m- good. I love it. I've had to deliver a lot of pizzas to afford that baby but she is mine all mine. I got it at the beginning of the summer. July 9th to be exact." Bernerd drawled in his best Translyvanian.

"I didn't know that you have a job." I said. I am learning a lot that I didn't know on this day that will not seem to end.

"I know Addie." And there was that definitive voice again. The one that says everything and knows everything and that you can probably trust with your life.

"Bernerd. Thanks. I can sleep now. Maybe I will see you tomorrow." I feel almost like bowing as I leave the room. Not in deference to Bernerd or anything. This moment feels like an ending or something, like the moment before the curtain comes down and all you can hear is thundering applause.

I wake up to the sun trying to poke its head through Sigge's window. Soft music is playing on her clock radio and I wonder what time it is. I roll over to see the clock and notice that Sigge is already out of her room and somewhere else in the house, giggling, in the distance. I am distracted by Sigge's absence so I don't notice the time. It's a good thing that I am lying down. The clock says 4:30 and it's not in the morning. You could knock me over with a feather if I wasn't already horizontal. The sun is actually trying to escape.

I pull myself out of bed and head for Sigge's closet. I pick out a t-shirt and sweat pants to borrow so that I can say good morning and good bye at the same time but not still wearing my pyjamas. I make my way into Sigge's bathroom.

121

On the counter to the left of the sink is a painting of a sun on a card done in oranges and yellows and gold glitter. I pick it up and read the inside:

Good morning sunshine. Hope you had a good sleep and that your snoring didn't keep you awake. (kidding) See you when you make it downstairs. Thanks for coming over last night. Having you here made me feel so much better.

Luv ya, Sig

ps. The little blue travel toothbrush and toothpaste on the counter are for you.

Can you believe how nice these Baxter people are considering that they are harbouring a known felon? I look at my self in the mirror and watch as two tears roll down the cliff of my cheeks and land on the counter. I have to pull myself together before I leave Sigg's room, so I wash my face with cold water and a loofah. If nothing else I will have a buffed and puffed complexion for my mug shots. I pull on the clothes that I have borrowed, pick my stuff up off of the floor and stride as confidently as I can across the room to the door. I take a deep breath, open the door to the sound of another of Sigge's giggles and a familiar voice that freezes my heart in my chest and my feet to the floor. The only sound I don't hear is the jingle of hand-cuffs.

122

"Addie? What are you doing? Contemplating a double reverse nose dive in the pike position down the stairs for yet another dramatic entrance?" barks Bernerd from behind me, making me lurch for the banister.

"Cute Bern. I guess I deserved that. But no. Not today. Who is downstairs with your parents and Sigge?" I ask, stalling for time. I know who is down there but I am not completely ready to face them.

"Okay Addie. Tell you what," says Bernerd with sparks shooting from his eyes. "I will go downstairs first and make sure it's safe for you to enter."

Oh sure I think to myself. I can see it all now. Bernerd will make some wild trumpet fanfare with his kazoo and announce me like crazy. He is twinkling like his mother and his sister all of a sudden so I definitely cannot trust him to carve me a safe path. I will do it myself.

"Forget it Bernerd. I don't completely trust you yet. Let me go first." As I say this I thrust out my jaw, steel myself for the consequences, and realize that I have just been had. These Baxter's sure are tricky.

****

From the bottom of the stairs I can walk right into the living room. I can see a reflection of myself in the mirror that hangs above the sofa. I look nervous but otherwise just like me. I realize that if I can see me whoever is in the living room can also see me so that explains the pause in conversation. I have to get this over with, so, here I go. This is me going into the living room. This is me holding my breath. This is me saying

"Hi Daddy."

And this is the Baxter's saying

"Cliff, Addie, You two need to talk. When you are done and if you are interested let us order in Chinese for dinner." And with those words we are left alone.

"Addie, you certainly had a good sleep. You must have needed it sweet-pea. What happened last night darlin'? Can you tell your old dad?"

" 'Daaaad' You know exactly what happened. I can't believe you are being so nice. Where is mom? Is she all right? Is she completely angry with me? Are you going to ground me?"

"Your mother is at home dear, and she is, um, as fine as you can expect. Cute as a bug, she is, but, you know, a little chagrined, I believe is the word. She wishes that things had turned out differently last night, for all of us, but they didn't. And no, you are not grounded, your mother is," and my dad snickers.

I found it hard to stifle the smirk that was pulling at my face. My mom is right. My dad and I both have the same goofy sense of humour.

"I can't believe we are laughing at this Dad!" I said. "This is so serious and is nothing to laugh about. Mom needs help. I need help. You need help. I can't live like this anymore. It is so embarrassing and weird and I can't show my face around town if mom keeps on assaulting people. I'm lucky the Baxter's let me stay here. And you wonder why I don't have any friends. They are all scared of me, and well, us and it's just not right Dad. I am going to have to change schools because I am the flavour of the day as of Monday, and you know how rude Mr. Dixon was to mom? Lindsay is ten times worse and she'll make my life miserable and…"

My dad cut me off before I could babble any longer.

"Adelaide, my little copper penny girl. WE should go home and talk about this. The Baxter's need sustenance and they don't need our thoughts for food. Get it darlin'? Thoughts for food, food for thought? Gawd I kill myself."

"Dad I mean it! I am not going to put up with this behaviour any more. I can't always take mom to the movies to distract her. I can't keep taking her out for lunch. I can't come home when I have free blocks to clean and make sure she is breathing. She is not my job. She is my mother. She is your wife. We are nice people. WE need help. I can't go around stealing cars any more. And, if you aren't going to do something about it all, I am and I will. Now let's go home. I have tortured these people enough."

My dad lets me pull him toward the door and in creepy unison we say,

"Good-bye Baxters. Thank-you. See you all soon." As I open the door, the street light of a moon flickers on and my dad says,

"As far as your mother and I are concerned Adelaide, you just took the car out of park and it rolled down the driveway is all. And you can thank your friend's brother for noticing and putting on the parking brake. You are so lucky to have friends like them Addie. Very lucky."

I guess I can put my prison stripes away.

I guess the guy at Mike's Market is not the moron I thought he was. Now I owe him too. And that Bernerd, and that Sigge, ooboy, and even their mom and dad. Tricky people, very, very tricky people.

And who even knew?

20

Today, Sunday came and went with the wishful smell of roast beef and mashed potatoes. I wished for it but it never happened. No surprise really. I haven't left my room for most of the day, my dad watched golf and I listened to it through the heat register, my mom was absent in her room. I made tomato soup, ate it with mushy crackers, wondered why I was eating like an invalid in a nursing home and went back to my room to contemplate why I found a new pink cell-phone adorned with a neon yellow bow outside my bedroom door. This surprise smells like bribery or a rather bizarre invitation into the twenty first century. Either way I'll take it. I have been wanting one of these things for ages.

The last few days have been interesting. I have come to some revelations thanks to Sigge and her mom and her brother and her dad. I only spent one evening with them in the Baxter compound and it was like my brain was sucked out and replaced with a sponge. Or maybe I was ready to learn to think for myself. Or maybe those Baxters are very good teachers. Who knows? But I think I know what to do now. Tomorrow will be the test. Lindsay is always a challenge but I am sure she will be especially weird when she sees me at school in the morning. And, at school I will be. How else will I be able to fulfill my driver's education requirement if I don't go to school? I can run but I won't take the bus forever.

****

I decide that the best thing is to try and be as inconspicuous as possible today. I will not draw attention to myself by wearing any of my new clothes. I will go directly to my locker. I will go directly to class. I will not be late. I will be early. I will be really early. I will go to school at 7 a.m. and beat the crowds. This is one excellent plan.

****

My day begins with English with Ms. Ostrowski. She is so intense and she teaches like she means it. You don't like to not do your homework for Ms. O because you feel like you might hurt her feelings if you don't. We are studying King Lear right now and it is one cool play. It's too bad I haven't read too much of it before now. I'm actually enjoying it. The bell rings and jars me out of my book. I clench my teeth as the class starts to dribble in. Kristi, okay, no dirty looks, safe, Morgan, he's cool, lives nowhere near me, Sigge, yahoo a definite friend and she is smiling at me, and Rob, Rob major heart throb, is smiling at me. Er no, he's smiling at Kristi, another yess, okay, oh no, it's the Lindsay. The big weird lame, wait a minute, she is not saying a thing. Lindsay. She is actually looking at me, the real Lindsay and she doesn't even have one finely-filed incisor showing. What gives? This is creepy. Something doesn't feel completely right.

The P.A. system in the classroom spews static just before someone in the office is going to speak. The speaker itself seems to be clearing its round green fabric covered throat before a disembodied voice is thrown into the room. Today Mr. Deville's nasal stylings call out over our heads.

"Excuse me for interrupting your class Ms. Ostrowski, but could you please send THAT GIRL to Ms. Plunkett's office? Thanks."

With that, every female looks around the room trying to figure out if she is that girl. I know they are asking for me, because as soon as the announcement is made the hair on the back of my neck stands straight on end, as if I am being set up to be hit by lightning. And I begin to sweat as if the room is immediately a sauna. It is hard to remain anonymous when you single yourself out.

"Hey Addie, that's you they want. What did you do this weekend to get your bad self called down to the office? It is so unlike you." Ms. O. smiles and winks and giggles.

I know she was just trying to be nice and everything but it opens a can of worms that I would rather have left unopened.

As I peel my damp self out of my desk I hear the whispers start at the back of the room and skitter toward me like a pack of chattering squirrels. I have to get out of here as quickly as I can because that furry brain feeling is starting to overtake me and I might fall over and this is already an embarrassing situation.

Out of the corner of my quickly blurring eyes I see Sigge motioning to Ms. O. to see if she can come with me and in a nano-second Sig is there, behind me, sorta holding me up.

I can hear Sigge's calm steady voice. She says,

"Add, it's all good. One foot in front of the other, and in three you will be out of the classroom. One, two, annnnnnnnd three. See?" And the door closes behind me. "Now let's get you to Ms. Plunkett."

Ms. Plunkett is the drug and alcohol counsellor at our school. What could she want with me? I don't do drugs, I don't have too much to do with alcohol, really. I don't. Oh. I get it.

"Sigge, thanks," I say with growing confidence. " But you know what? I can take it from here. You rock by the way."

"Thanks, Addie. Bernerd, and me too, of course, think you rock too, by the way. Oh and Ms. Plunkett. She's awesome. Our family worked with her. You'll like her. I'll see you after school." And with that Sigge bounces back to class and leaves me with my mouth hanging open like a big mouth bass.

Now where did I leave that can of worms?

21

Ms. Plunkett's office is cosy for a school office. It is filled with plants and probably 7,000 Mr. Potato Head dolls in varying shapes and sizes. She even has a Mr. Potato Head floor lamp instead of overhead fluorescent lighting. She has replaced her boring office furniture with a fuzzy lime green couch and an orange arm chair with a leopard spotted fuzzy Snuggly, one of those blanket thingies with arms. I guess sometimes in a counsellor's office you might need a hug, so a blanket with arms makes sense, except you really could just wear your dressing gown backwards, but then again who has a dressing gown at school? Hugging yourself just isn't the same as getting a hug from someone else but sometimes you have no choice.

Ms. Plunkett is a bohemian. She has unruly naturally curly grey and black hair. She is wearing sandals with red work socks. She has on a long blue and yellow flowered dress with a red sweater that matches her socks. I guess you could call her style eclectic. I also like her glasses. They are perfect purple circles.

The air in here is warm and sweet. The scent of lavender and vanilla candles permeates the room. It feels as if there is sunshine seeping through the blinds, beam by beam. Until now I have never stepped inside this office. I have always walked right on past on my way out of the front door. There are usually so many of those lame-o weirdoes lined up outside of her office that I never want to venture in. Way too scary, and way too real.

"Hi Addie. I can call you Addie can't I? Or would you prefer Adelaide? Come on in and sit. I am going to make myself some tea. Would you like some?" Ms. Plunkett asks.

I sit on the farthest end of the couch away from her.

"Uh, um, no thanks. I am fine right now." I offer.

"So Addie, I hear you had a rather eventful weekend. Do you want to talk about it?" She tilts her head to the left and almost smiles.

"No. There is nothing to say. I over reacted that's all. Do you need something else from me? I have to get home." I say as confidently as I can.

"No Addie, not now. But I would like to see you again tomorrow. I'll come and get you from Ms. Ostrowski's English class at ten. Alright?" Ms. Plunkett stares right at me.

"Actually? What for? I am good, really. There is no need to come and get me. That's too weird. Plus, what do you need to see me for? What do you want to talk to me about? My grades are good and my attendance is almost perfect." I argue and stare at a point directly in the middle of her forehead. *No point in making real eye contact.*

"Fine. I won't come and get you Addie but you can do me a favour and come to my group session tonight? It's a great opportunity to talk about what bugs you and maybe get a little insight into things, possibly figure out why you sometimes over react."

"Are you kidding me? From all the skids and low-lifes? What can they offer me? Instructional and motivational materials on intravenous drug use? Thanks but no thanks Ms. P. I am good. I am fine. Really. WOW." I snap, and then reconsider stamping my foot.

"Okay Addie it is settled. I can either get you from class tomorrow at ten or I can come to your house today after school to chat with you and your family." Ms Plunkett is nothing if not insistent. *Where have I seen this behaviour before? Why does it seem so familiar?*

whine. "I surrender. Where and when tonight, Ms. Plunkett?" I

Anything, ANYTHING but a home visit.

"7:30 pm in the Annex. See you there. Oh and when you get back to class could you send Dakota down to see me please?" she says as if this is a real conversation and not a bamboozlement.

"Yeah, sure," I say, "No problem," even though I am really puzzled. Dakota Duncan is the coolest most perfect kid in my grade. She is cute and smart and funny. What could Ms. Plunkett possibly want with her?

My walk home is slower and much longer than usual. I am taking the long-cut apparently. Leaves crunch under my heels and the smell of wood smoke from late afternoon fires tickles my nose. The smell is a comfort and a wish. I wish we had a fireplace. `I could stare into the flames and watch them predict my future. I love the smell. It is the scent of Thanksgiving dinner and pumpkin pies of "yore". I speak Elizabethan when I am feeling nostalgic. Darn you Ms. O!

As I reach the end of our driveway I can hear The Rolling Stones -- (I Can't Get No) Satisfaction blaring from the open front door. From here I can see my mother dancing like one of those caged go-go girls in the living room. She should be in a cage. She is wild and flailing and way too much for me

137

to handle. I will go to Brewster's for coffee then to school for 7:30. I will text Sigge and see if she can meet me. I spin on my toes and aim myself toward Brewster's. (I hope mom didn't notice me. Right. As if.) Oh moon. Where are you? Can you smile your sardonic little smirk down on me please? Your distance and your cool remove are what I need right now. Everything is too close, too tightly wound around my heart and brain that I need a sense of being watched over but not squished and smothered.

With that wish the street-lights come on. When I was a little kid when the street lights came on I knew that I had to go home. Now when the street lights come on it's a signal NOT to go home. I honestly thought the weekend would have woken my mom up to the reality of her situation. That she would have learned something, that she would realize that she has become a huge embarrassment to me. I am so stupid. I can't believe I was sucked in again.

"Sigge. Meet at Brewster's in 10." I text and wait.

I walk into Brewster's and breathe in the aroma of freshly ground coffee beans. It too is a warm and comforting smell. It appears I am seeking out warmth and comfort today. Why does it have to be anywhere but at home? The sound of wind chimes on my phone informs me that Sigge has replied.

"No can do Addelicious. Appointment Important. C U demain." Great. Bernerd maybe?

"Hey. Sigge bailed on me. Can I buy you java?"

The sound of ducks quacking announces Bernerd's text.

"Sorry Addie. Not tonight. Commitment. Bye U."

Okay. I am completely, unequivocally alone. There is nothing left to do except go to the stupid meeting. How lame am I, alone and eagerly anticipating a "fun-time" meeting with all of the local losers? Hmmmm. What exactly does this say about me? I will savour and sip my mocha slowly. I will adopt a serene expression, moon-like, removed. I am Addie-Zen. Cool, collected and totally in control.

23

What is worse than walking into a room full of strange and weird people? Nothing unless you walk into a room full of strange and weird people and watch as your mother clocks your neighbour in the jaw. Nothing these people have experienced will be as crazy and deranged as my weekend. I am not so enthusiastic about being here but I can't and won't go home, Oscar at Brewster's wanted to close so, here I am in "The Annex." It sounds like a room where they keep old furniture and broken things. Actually it kinda does contain broken things, in the form of people I guess.

The double doors open inward into the room. I will make an entrance. I will kick the doors open and jump into the room and adopt a ninja stance. I will attack the air with fists of fire. I will demonstrate the Addie strength and power that I know I possess. I will collect myself and smooth out my wrinkled clothes with damp palms and stride confidently to a chair, any chair, and sit, like the confident, cool, serene child of the moon that I am.

"Excuse me, um, are trying to open those doors with your mind?" a very cute boy with fabulous eyelashes says to me with a lop-sided smile.

Ohmigaawd. How long have I been standing in front of the door pretending I am a ninja? I find myself smoothing my shirt and touching my hair and sweating and staring but saying nothing.

I am the personification of awkward. I am awkward on feet.

"My name is Matthew and your feet are frozen to the floor it seems. Let me open the door and I will inspect the place. I will make sure it is perfect for your entrance. Excuse me whilst I open yon door. Oh sorry. I have a tendency to lapse into Elizabethan since my English teacher got a hold of me."

"Ms. O. perhaps?" I croak and smile.

"Yep. Block C. English 10." Matthew informs me. "I love that class. Come on in mystery person….."

"Nah. It's okay. I'm not sure I'm gonna hang around." I mutter. I feel my ears are red and burning.

It is probably safe to go home. It's almost 7:30 and my dad is probably walking in the door right this very second. I should go and help him make dinner. I don't need to be here. I want to be home. I need to be home. I need my room. I need to hang upside down and talk to the moon.

"Addie, hello! I am so happy you were able to make it." Ms. Plunkett chirps and puts a hand on my shoulder. "Come on in and sit and stay a while."

"Um," I say as I am jolted away from my thoughts, "I think I will just wait and see you tomorrow. I'd really like to go home now."

"But you are here now dear. Give us fifteen minutes of your time and if you really can't take any more of us you can go. You made the effort to be here, so what the heck? However, if you really must go I understand and I will see you tomorrow like we planned, at 10." Ms. Plunkett drifts through the door into The Annex on a lavender soaked cloud of perfume.

Fifteen minutes can't hurt, I guess.

24

I enter "The Annex" and see a circle of ten chairs. There is no pit to sacrifice newcomers so I relax. In the room, so far, is eyelash boy, Ms. Plunkett and me. Egad. This is so embarrassing. I will just pick a chair and sit and not make eye contact. If I pretend I am not here then no one else will be able to see me.

The door opens again and again. Everyone you would expect to be here is here. The Goth and Emo kids who smoke and wear dog collars and who skulk behind the school have arrived. They are pale skinned, virtually transparent. I suspect they listen to the theme song from The Exorcist on repeat on their ipods . And then there are the other kids, the walking on sunshine types, the popular, the regular and the darlings of the school that I never expected to see here because they bubble with life. This really is so freakin' weird.

I find myself looking at my hands, back and front. My nails have disappeared. Chewed to the quick. I am not sure exactly when that happened. Weird.

I hear the door opening and closing but I do not look up. My hands seem way more important right now. I can, however, tell that the room is filling up with people because there is no longer an echo in here and it is getting hot, and humid and hard to breathe.

A distinguished looking but casually dressed man with a rather ironic moustache has arrived and has taken the seat next to me. I pretend not to notice him. Ms. Plunkett plunks herself on the other side of me and clears her throat. I am trapped.

"Ahem. Hi! Good evening everyone! It's great to see all of you in this room tonight. Thank-you for making the time to be here. We have a new person joining us and I would love you all to make Addie feel welcome."

Great. A whole room of needy.

A chorus of heys and hi's circle around to greet me. Some are less enthusiastic than others but what do I expect, a

145

red freakin' carpet? Just as I nod my own hellos the annex doors swing open and in walk Sigge and Bernerd. *I can't believe what I am seeing. Sigge and Bernerd have come here to support me. What amazing friends they are. They didn't have to do this and look at that. They are both chatting away as if being BFFs to the world was their main concern in life. I am so lucky. But wait, how did they know I was here?*

"Okay people. Let's get started and get everyone to do their emotional check-in. Andrea? How are you feeling this week?"

Andrea looks up through her curtain of blue hair and says, "Seven".

"So Ms. Andrea. Do you feel the need to talk just now or would you like us to get back to you? That seven has been pretty consistent. Well done!"

"You can get back to me Ms. Plunkett. I am just happy to be here. Thanks."

Are you kidding me? Happy to be HERE? No way. Really?

"Matthew? How about you?"

"Well Ms. Plunkett, Dr. Rubin, I am, right now anyway, a nine. Dad is in overcompensation mode and I am making the most of his generosity and time. We went to a couple of movies and bought some video games that I have been wanting, and the best part is we actually have some real groceries in the house. Right now, he's coping and I have my dad again for a while anyway. I can't say it's all great because I know this won't last, he's getting that cranky, anxious edge to his voice, but for now he and I are okay."

"Nice work Matthew. I can see that you have been doing your homework and listening to your dad and yourself. Any other comments?" offers Dr. Rubin.

"Matthew -- Whoa man! -- Major change! Good on you guys."

Perry Adler, one of the emo kids and the son of the wealthiest dermatologist in town, smiles and offers Matthew this encouragement. I haven't seen Perry smile since Kindergarten. *This whole scene is so bizarre. Why would a guy like Perry be here? He has everything. His family is perfect. He may look tragic but his family is not, is it?*

"Thanks, Perry," Matthew acknowledges, "really. Thanks for the phone support."

Phone support? What the what? How can Perry Adler help anyone? He wears black lipstick for heaven sake. These people I guess I don't really know are very surprising. This whole thing is starting to feel like some wacky twelve step hoo-haw cult.

The kids are all checking in with pretty high scores tonight it seems. They're so mature and adult and rather robotic. My parents could take a lesson! There is one person who does not speak though. Their head is encased in a charcoal grey hoody doing their best imitation of the grim reaper. No face, just dark eyeless shadow. Kinda creepy actually. But most everyone else seems relaxed and I am surprised and completely pissed off. They all have beautiful, perfect lives. Either they are smart or beautiful, or come from perfectly normal beautiful homes with perfectly normal beautiful parents. It's easy for them to be relaxed. This evening is a social event, a gathering where they can compare their perfection. What do they know about velour fathers and drunken nude mothers? Why are they even here? Geez. No! Why am I even here? I am suddenly aware of a Sesame Street song playing in my head, "one of these things is not like the other...."

As the circle gets closer to Sigge and Bernerd, Bernerd starts to look a little pale. I feel badly to put him through this ordeal. Neither he nor Sigge should have to listen to all this emotional crap. They don't need to be a part of a Silverwoods underbelly that isn't.

"Bernerd? How about you? What is your emotional temperature this evening?" asks Ms. Plunkett.

Bernerd has not seemed himself since he walked in. I know he is going to talk about my drama infliction and how I kept him and his family up till all hours and that I wrecked his weekend and, *"Oh man. I am so sorry Bernerd, Sigge. You guys are amazing. Thanks for being here but really. I am okay. I am going to leave right now. Let's all go -- let's get out of this place. Let's go for burgers. Come on. Let's go. We don't belong here."* My stomach is churning as I wish I could just blurt this all out but I can't and I don't. I will sit here, still and bitchy and let everyone of these liars tell their pathetic, silly little stories about how they didn't get the perfect party dress or dog collar and that their lives are ruined forever. What do they know? You would think that Ms. Plunkett and Dr. Rubin would have better things to do on a Monday night than listen to spoiled, perfect people complain. Monday Night Football anyone?

I can hear Bernerd's voice but I haven't been looking at either he or Sigge. I am too embarrassed about what they will say. This is all so awkward. I sneak a glance toward them and notice Sigge is holding Bernerd's hand. That is so like her. She is so incredibly supportive of her friends and especially her family. But I get that. Her family is easy to support and love. They're PERFECT.

Bernerd's words start to dribble into my ears.

"I got a call this morning on my cell, from Eric. I can tell he's tweakin'. He's talking all crazy about how he had to drop out of university because his professors knew he had the formula to reverse carbon capture. He's asking me for money because he needs to support his research into the brain activity of monkeys. Meth gets Eric so crazy and wired up. Then he says that if I don't help him he will come and mess me up, steal my scooter, break into the house and sell dad's art collection and then I'll be sorry for not telling him our new address. When I say no he tells me to F right off and hangs up. He does this every couple of months and today of all days he had to call. It's not as if this was a quiet and Zen-filled weekend. Normally I can handle his drug-addled nonsense but he caught me at a weak moment. So that's why I am a two. But, actually, saying all of that out loud feels way better."

I see Sigge relax her grip on Bernerd's hand and sorta smile at him.

"I am so sorry he always calls you, Bern. But I can't talk to him anymore. It's his problem not mine, not yours, not mom and dad's. You are the one with the giant ears and an even bigger heart. And you have mom's old cell number. Lucky you!" Sigge smirks her signature smirk and Bernerd winks at her. Andrea pipes up,

"Bernerd don't listen to your sister. Your ears are just fine!" A soft giggle circles the circle. "Your heart shouldn't be filled with guilt. Eric's should. If he could feel."

"Thanks Andrea. I know it's his problem, but sometimes he tries to make it mine, and sometimes he rattles me. Like this time." Bernerd clears some anger from his throat.

Eric? Who is Eric? Why do I not know Eric? Sigge has a secret Eric in her life. Sigge has a secret from me? Actually?

"Thank- you Bernerd. Your continued patience with your brother is admirable but something we need to work on and explore. Would you like to add anything else tonight?" queries Dr. Rubin.

"Nah. I am good for now. I have had my spotlight moment. Which reminds me, the following is a commercial for the spring production! Bram Stoker's "Dracula" starring me

151

will be on stage in four months. Rumour has it I will be fantastic!" Bernerd's smile lights up the room.

"I have no doubt about that at all Bernerd." acknowledges Dr. Rubin.

"Now that brings us to our newcomer Addie. How are you feeling tonight Addie? On a scale of one to ten, one being crappy and 10 being as happy as you can be under the circumstances, where would you say you were?" questions Ms. Plunkett.

I lower my eyes to the ground. My ears are on fire and my palms are sweating. Everyone is expecting me to be sad and weak. I shake my head "no" and proceed to count the stripes on Perry's pant leg. Then I make a decision.

It's time to go home.

"I, my friends, am an 'effin' twelve. Things are perfect in my world. I am not one of you people. I am really perfect. I am fine. I am just freakin' fine."

I say all of this as I stomp toward the exit. I notice no one is looking at all surprised by my "moment" No one is running after me.

No one is saying *"Addie, Addie dear. It's all right. I won't break the dishes against the wall again. I won't throw shoes at you when we disagree about laundry detergent. I won't do anything again darlin'. Really. I won't. I promise."* I watch myself open the door and step into the hallway of the annex. I lean against the wall and love the coolness of it on the small of my back. The silence is huge and very dramatic. I am small and really uber pathetic. I hear the clacking of shoe heels crossing the floor to the door, slowly but deliberately. I expect to see Sigge's face but Dr. Rubin peers around the door as he opens it. He smiles and says,

"Hey Addie. You okay to get home on your own my friend, or would you like a ride?"

"No I don't NEED a ride. Do you think I am incapable of walking home by myself? There is no need to underestimate me Dr. Rubin. I am just fine. I can walk the five blocks to my house without any help. Thank-you and good night." And with my last pronouncement Dr. Rubin pulls his head back through the open door and disappears into the annex.

I need silence and the sanctuary of my room. I need some fresh air. I need all of these wackos to leave me alone.

The car is not in the driveway. The house is completely dark. The Rolling Stones are totally unsatisfied and still singing about it on repeat. A note on the kitchen table under the empty crantini pitcher says "We have flown this coop and gone to "The Nest" for dinner. Hah! I kill myself. Love, Daddy-O". Thankfully mes parents didn't include me in their dinner reservation. "The Nest" is a hangout for the geriatric martini crowd and hanging with the blue hairs is definitely not something that I have pencilled into my agenda. I put the empty pitcher into the dishwasher, wipe the table and throw the note into the garbage. I ascend the stairs to my room, two steps at a time. Peace awaits.

Finally. Safe. Sound. Enclosed. My completely delicious womb of a room. The furnace is groaning and whispering to my curtains. They flutter and dance in response to its warm breath attention. The clouds have cleared in my head and the moon is peering cautiously through the bottom corner of my window. I make it nervous it seems. It peeks in to see if I am still awake, still breathing. It demonstrates some parental concern. It is looking paler than usual tonight. It seems worried.

I plop myself down on the bed and send a text to Sigge. This new-fangled device is amazing.

"ERIC?"

I wait to hear back. I thought Sigge and Bernerd were there for me tonight. I thought they wanted to help me! They were there for themselves though. Secrets are everywhere, and very difficult to keep. They are a heavy burden to carry in your pocket and they scream to be shared sometimes. Like last weekend I guess. Whoa. A secret Eric. A secret drunk mother. Who knew? But I guess that is the point. No one is supposed to know. I can't believe that I am so self-absorbed that I don't even hear my friends have issues too! Impossible. Am I not paying close enough attention to the details of our conversations? The moon seems to be nodding at me. It is not as pale as it was when I came in here. It's hearing my thoughts and it is acknowledging my failings as a friend. Back - off moon. I thought you understood. I thought you were my friend.

I heave myself up from my bed and close the curtains. Furiously whip them closed actually. How dare the moon comment! This is my room. This is my private sea of tranquility. This is where I am right and where I am safe. How dare you moon!

Oh man. I am railing. I am doing a King Lear without a heath.

I open my curtains slowly and a little sheepishly. The moon is shrouded by a thick fog and I can't see it clearly. It avoids me.

"Come back, please, Moon.

I need you. I am sorry for yapping at you.

I know you are right but it's hard to say it to you out loud."

Wind chimes announce Sigge's text.

"Another day-o, friend-o."

She responds and almost immediately a text follows from Bernerd.

"It's not only the shadows that know....mwahaha."

I can tell she is tired and Bernerd is Bernerd. The clouds clear a little and the moon takes a chance and looks at me sideways.

"I'll talk to you later," I say, "when I am cooler, more perfectly calm and completely collected. Good night my cul de sac moon."

Ohmigawd. Did you hear me say that? I can't believe I said that out loud. How sick and sappy sweet. It is just a streetlamp, it can't solve my problems, it is just a fake stupid moon and I am just a fake stupid kid.

Good Night Moon.

****

Morning comes like it does, slow, fuzzy, and with regret.

I will wear flannel pyjamas to school today. No point to getting all dolled up. I will put my hair in a pony, pull on a cloud grey hoody and slink to school. Sigge can catch up to me if she wants. I am sure to get an earful about my performance last night. I don't think Ms. Plunkett will ignore it either. I will no doubt see her at ten.

I jump down the stairs into the kitchen. I can see a missing homework assignment on the table with a wet drink ring and crumbs imbedded into it. How can I hand this in? My mom has used my English essay as a flippin' coaster. OMG. I grab the essay from the table, stuff it into my bag and catch a glimpse of myself in the chrome side of the toaster.

"Who's the skid?" flashes through my head. I look just like the human crow dumpster divers I see downtown. Grey is the color of pavement and my sad dead eyes. Great country song lyrics. But you know what? I am not going to worry about how I look just now. I don't have time to be lame. I've got to get to school. I have got to get out of this place before the partiers awake and descend.

****

Walking is supposed to be therapeutic but the October puddles capture images of me on their surface. I see a very different vision of myself in them than what I saw on the weekend. I was beautiful then and hopeful and filled with color. Today I am a pencil grey thin outline of a person, who is

158

empty on the inside. I am back to where I was early last week, before the color. Miserable and itchy. Okay. What is going on here? I can't shake this nasty empty feeling. Usually walking away from the house helps, but not today. My heart is trying to escape my chest, my ears are making a strange wocka -wocka sound and I am breathing as if I have run for miles. I am going to pass out. I have to get to school. I have to get to school. I have to get myself to school. One foot in front of the other Adelaide, one foot in front of the other and you will make it. Concentrate on the cracks. Stomp on them. Stomp on them good. Stomp like you mean it. Stomp. Stomp! STOMP! Stomp on the cracks and break your mother's back.... Ohmigawd! I should never have played that game as a kid.

The inside of the school at this time of day is calm and serene. There is no one around except the happiest Hawaiian-shirted, one-armed janitor in the world, Mr. Moore. The kids call him Bill "the Fugitive" Moore but not to his face. By this time of the morning he is in his dungeon drinking a giant tub of coffee and watching sports highlights on his mini television. Because my head is down I notice what a great job Bill is doing on the floor. It sparkles. Maybe I will compliment him later. No I won't. That would be weird. My locker is just around the corner to the left. I can't believe the shine on these floors. Truly a mirror-like finish. It's unfortunate I am marring his perfect floor with wet sneaker tracks and water droplets.

Before I have a chance to actually peel my eyes off of the floor and onto my lock, a pair of eyes beautifully made up in dark eye-liner and sparkles are looking at me from the floor.

"Hey Addie!" a voice says.

"Oh hey, Dakota. Nice eye make-up. I noticed it in the reflection on the floor. Can you believe "the fugitive" can actually get concrete to look like a mirror? What are you doing here so early?"

"I just had to escape my house. This is the safest place I know." she confesses.

Is this some alternate universe? Cute and perfect Dakota Duncan is talking to me like her equal. She is always nice to everyone though. But today she is talking to me like I understand her, like we are friends or something. Like she thinks I am special. Yea. Right.

"Escape? Are you okay?" I ask and look at her with saucer eyes. *Boy is she speaking my language. But really, what could Dakota have to escape?*

"Oh yeah. I forgot. You left the meeting before you heard what happened to me yesterday morning. I am still freaked out. You have no idea. My mom is wandering around like a zombie and I keep hearing sirens and having visions of my dad doing the walk of shame into the cop car so coming to school is the healthiest and cheeriest option." Dakota visibly shudders. AND Ms. Plunkett is here."

"Wait a minute, Dakota. Hang on. You were at that meeting last night? You? Seriously?" I sputter, almost choking on my hard-edged embarrassment. "I didn't see you." *This is awkward.*

"Yup. I was there. I was sitting right beside Dr. Rubin. You really know how to make an exit." Dakota smiles and isn't the least bit mean or sarcastic or anything. "Everyone has one of those moments, eventually, in group. It's okay. We all get it. We've all been there. Anger is the first step in healing."

Dakota was the grim reaper wannabe. OMG. This is so weird and so predictable. There is always the unexpected cute kid with a problem in teen angsty stories. Why should my story be any different? If this was an after school movie we would end up as best friends. But this is no movie, it's my stinkin' lame-o life and me and Dakota Duncan will say hi in the halls and that is it. But whoa, it's still pretty weird.

161

"Oh. Um. Well, I uh, I don't have anything to heal. I don't think I will be going back to that group. I don't think I need...."

"I know, I know," she interjects, "I just want to let you know, though, that if you need anything, conversation, coffee, a shoulder, that I can supply any and all. Sorry you're having a hard time, or not, with whatever. Here's my cell number. Anytime is fine. Take care, Addie. See you." Dakota hands me a neon pink sticky star note. Her silhouette walks away from me toward the light from the window at the end of the hallway. *How symbolically angelic. I could just puke.* I stick the note on the inside of my locker door. Maybe I will call her sometime, who knows. But probably not. I'd really like to know what she said in group after I left though. *Dakota Duncan. In group. Weird. Sigge and Bernerd are in group. I really need to think about this. Dakota seems so nice, so warm, so trusting. Sigge and Bernerd seem so sane, so helpful; the whole family seems to know everything.....*

"Addie? Is that you? You are here awfully early." Ms. Plunkett and her shoes clickety- clack toward me. "It was good to see you last night. Hope you enjoyed meeting everyone."

"Oh gee, Ms. P. I am so sor..." I start to apologize but am cut off mid-sentence.

"No explanations or excuses needed Addie. It's how you were feeling. We get it. I am glad that I caught you so early because I just wanted to let you know that I won't be able to meet with you this morning at ten. You can come and schedule another appointment for another day or you can come to group on Monday night or not. Your choice. I just came in to collect a few documents and Dakota and head out again. See you soon I hope." And off Ms. Plunkett toddles down the shiny hall toward her office.

I have a new emptiness in my chest. I had absolutely no desire to go and talk to Ms. Plunkett today. I figured that she was going to come and haul me out of class and embarrass me about last night and now that she can't meet with me, I am disappointed. Jeez. I don't get it. I don't get any of this at all.

I slide down the outside of the lockers and sit on the floor. I trace the deliberate artistic cracks in the concrete with my finger. I pretend the cracks are rivers and that they are running feverishly to the sea. They move so quickly that they do not have time to think about what they are running from. I imagine how the spray from the fast moving water feels as it hits my face and am jarred back into school reality when I realize my face really is wet. I look up onto the striped pant leg of Perry Adler and the tip of his soggy purple umbrella.

Perry folds his umbrella and snaps the closure into place. He shakes off the excess water before he places his "brolly" into his locker. He is completely, on purpose, ignoring me.

"Hi Perry," I mouth as I tug on his pant leg. He pops one of his earphones out, looks down at me, and gives me a kick in the shin before he shuffles down the hall.

"That's for never letting me be Batman!" he yells over his shoulder as he makes his way toward the music room. "You are one stubborn woman!" With that declaration he and his black smile-less lips and broken kindergarten heart disappear down the hall.

"Hey!" I yell at the back of Perry's head while stifling a nasty expletive. "Dude! Wowch! Actually? You kicked me? Really? You're kidding right?"

Perry Adler is a big jerk! That kick really hurt. Now I know why he hasn't smiled for the past ten years. Batman envy. A subtle creeping insidious envy that destroys all who experience it apparently. Geez. Did he really have to kick me? That's just downright mean and nasty. No wonder he's in group.

Okay now, Ms. Adelaide Blanche Sinclair, let's re-cap. Perry Adler is crabby and scary and very un-nice. Dakota Duncan has some issues. Sigge and Bernerd and their parents have a secret Eric. You have parents who are alcoholics and one of those said parents is also a drug addict. All five of you are in group. You are all in group for a reason. The group helps people become reason-able, except for Perry obviously. The group helps people. The group helps some people. Maybe I need "some" help, just a little help. Maybe. I'll see. I'll go and see one more time. I will find out what happened with Dakota. I am really curious and well, kinda nosey, about what she said. I will be pissed off at my parents for making me keep heavy secrets. I will look forward to wearing my new clothes again, when the time and the color is right. I will call Lindsay in two years, no point rushing into being tortured. I will be Lucy in the Spring Production. I will drive into the night, with the moon on my shoulder, the wind in my hair and only one or two teenage troubles in my purse, but not right now, in a couple of months. Now it's English with Ms. O and she will just have to do. Oh and one last thing...

"Excuse me, Bill, um, Mr. Moore?" I say as he pokes his head out from his custodian's dungeon, "I notice that you did an amazing job on the floors this weekend. I am so not kidding.... Nice work. Really. Seriously. Beautiful. Thanks." Mr. Moore looks a little stunned at the compliment but also pleased that someone is actually paying attention for a change. That someone actually noticed. That someone actually cares, you know, about his floor.